"Will ... **to** ...

Robyn heard the husk...

Nick nodded, his green-eyed gaze flicking between her and the room in the Mexican villa where she was holding him hostage.

Robyn slid the key into the left handcuff and released it. Slowly Nick slipped his hand out. Then, in one swift motion, he captured her wrist and pulled her onto his lap. She gasped in dismay, but he pinned her hands between them. Just that fast, she was trapped!

"You said you wouldn't try anything!" Color streamed into Robyn's cheeks.

Nick's lips curved in a parody of a smile. "I lied."

Dear Reader,

American Romance's tenth-anniversary celebration continues....

For the past three months, we've been bringing you some of your favorite authors, and some brand-new ones, in exciting promotions. In its decade, American Romance has launched the careers of over forty writers and made stars of a dozen more.

Cathy Gillen Thacker is one of them. She has been with American Romance from the very beginning, and in the past ten years has penned almost forty books.

A full-time novelist, Cathy once taught piano to children. She and her husband have three children and, after moving cross-country several times, now live in Texas.

We hope you've enjoyed our special tenth-anniversary selections. And we look forward to many more anniversaries of success....

Sincerely,

Debra Matteucci
Senior Editor & Editorial Coordinator

Cathy Gillen Thacker

KIDNAPPING NICK

Harlequin Books

TORONTO • NEW YORK • LONDON
AMSTERDAM • PARIS • SYDNEY • HAMBURG
STOCKHOLM • ATHENS • TOKYO • MILAN
MADRID • WARSAW • BUDAPEST • AUCKLAND

Published October 1993

ISBN 0-373-16506-4

KIDNAPPING NICK

Printed in U.S.A.

Prologue

Nick Wyatt felt as if he were floating. Taking a magic carpet ride on an incredibly soft, incredibly warm bed. Only the bed was moving. Shifting against him. Warmly.

He was used to motion. As a race-car driver, he experienced top speeds and smooth-as-silk rides every day. But this—this was something else, something he'd never felt. He struggled to open his eyes. It seemed an impossible feat. Almost as impossible as the soft feminine laughter he heard in his ears as the bed shifted again. And then again. More warmth. More laughter. More shifting of the bed. Then the sensation of coolness as the sheet was ripped from the length of him.

Nick groaned and reached blindly for the sheet. He was so tired. The race at Daytona had worn him out. All he wanted was to sleep. But that was impossible, with the girlish giggling going on around him.

"C'mon, Nicky," a soft voice urged as someone wetly kissed his ear. Hands tugged at his Jockey shorts, drawing them down over his legs. "Wake up, sweetheart." The hands moved back up, caressing now. "That's a boy, wake up now."

Nick tried again and this time managed to get his eyes open. The room was spinning like a ride at the Six Flags Amusement park back home in Dallas. Everything was a fuzzy blur. He felt as if he were looking through a veil, and his mouth tasted like cotton.

"Ah, see, girls?" the soft voice purred triumphantly. "He's waking up, just like I told you he would."

Nick blinked again, sure he was dreaming. He had to be. There was no way *this* could be real. He hadn't gone to bed...

"That's right, Nick," a low male voice coaxed.

His head pounding, his muscles tensing warily, Nick turned in the direction of the sound just in time to see a man and a camera.

Nick swore profusely and grabbed for the sheet.

"Say cheese!"

Chapter One

Nick Wyatt shifted restlessly in his seat as the Dallas Symphony finished the third movement of Beethoven's *Ninth*. Classical music was okay, but it wasn't his favorite. Given his choice, he'd much rather have attended a Van Halen concert. But his mother had insisted, saying she wouldn't talk family business with him until after the concert and the postconcert party given by the members of the Symphony League, of which she was currently chairwoman. So it looked to be a long night.

If not for the extremely beautiful woman beside him, Nick would have considered the whole night a loss. But, he thought, smiling, it was hardly a loss when a woman that gorgeous was seated next to you. Her hair was a rich sable brown, and it tumbled away from her face and fell to her shoulders in soft, loose waves. Her mouth—stained the same scarlet as the floor-length red velvet evening cloak she wore—was sexy as hell, her lips full, perfectly proportioned and bow shaped. The golden glow of her skin lent her an exotic aura he found very compelling, as did the oval shape of her face, the straight prominence of her nose and the subtly carved bones of her cheeks. As for the rest of her, Nick knew she was tall and slim, but he couldn't see much of her beaded evening dress, because she had kept her cloak on. He wondered why she hadn't taken it off, especially since she looked to be a little warm, then chalked it up to the fact she had arrived late and probably didn't want to disturb the patrons on either side of her during the concert.

The movement ended to thunderous applause. The lights came up, signaling the start of intermission, and the woman turned to him with a smile, for the first time revealing the shape and color of her eyes. They were the same rich sable brown as her hair, long lashed and framed by thick, arched, dark sable brows. They also shimmered with intelligence, and that was a combination Nick never had been able to resist—intelligence and beauty.

Her smile widened as her eyes lit up in recognition. "You're Nick Wyatt, aren't you?" she asked softly.

Nick was used to being recognized. As one of the top race-car drivers in the country, his picture was often on the sports pages, and again in ads for the motor oil company that acted as his sponsor. He leaned close enough to inhale the warm floral scent of her perfume. He couldn't take his eyes off her. "How did you know?" This woman did not look as if she hung out at the track, and she sure as heck wasn't any driver groupie....

"I know your mother."

Which meant, Nick decided, that she was a society babe, probably into good works. The kind of woman who looked down her pretty little nose at what Nick did to earn a living. The kind who would never understand why he'd given up an executive position with the family company to test himself and the state-of-the-art cars he was privileged enough to drive. But she was intriguing nonetheless. Very intriguing. "Through the Symphony League?" he asked.

"And various other good works."

His gaze moved down to her mouth and lingered before returning to her eyes. "You're a socialite then?"

She frowned, as if insulted, and murmured, "I hate that word. It's so old-fashioned." She stood without answering his question.

It was what she looked like though, Nick thought. Rich, pampered, used to getting what she wanted out of life, and the opposite sex. Just like him. He found that thought appealing. He liked a challenge, and this woman, this very beautiful woman, presented one hell of a challenge.

Drawing her cloak more closely around her, she said, "I think I'll go out and get something to drink during the intermission."

"I'll join you," Nick said, and was pleased to find she was receptive to the idea.

His steps light and purposeful, he followed her up the aisle. Once out in the lobby, however, she bypassed the concessions and headed for the exit doors.

Outside, people were standing in small groups, smoking and chatting. Curious, because she didn't look like someone who had any vices, Nick followed her. The January wind blew right through his tuxedo. It had to be about thirty-five out there. There'd been a winter storm earlier in the week, and though the streets and sidewalks were now clear, snow still glittered white in the glow of the streetlights.

"Need a light?" Nick asked, wishing it wasn't so damn cold. Not that the weather seemed to be bothering her. Her cheeks were as rosy as the cloak she was wearing.

"No," she said. "I don't smoke."

"Neither do I." He paused. She was even more hauntingly beautiful in the moonlight. He rubbed his hands over his arms, generating as much warmth as he could. "Then why are we standing out here, freezing?" he teased.

She held his eyes with disturbing directness. "Because it's less crowded than in the lobby," she said.

True, Nick thought.

"Would you like to go somewhere to warm up?" she asked.

"Where?"

"You name it."

Nick blinked. "You're suggesting we skip the last half of the concert?"

She laughed at his stunned expression, then said flirtatiously, "You're telling me you'd mind?"

Nick grinned.

"I saw you snoozing away in there," she taunted.

"I wasn't asleep."

Her sable eyes glimmered speculatively. "But you wanted to be."

True again.

"So are we on?" she persisted.

Nick hesitated as every predatory instinct he had surged within him, tightening his gut and everything below the waist. "You wouldn't miss the second half?" He kept his eyes on her.

She shrugged insouciantly. "It won't be the last time they play Beethoven's *Ninth*."

Nick smiled. He liked the soft, smoky sound of her voice. "So what are we waiting for?"

A white stretch limo pulled up at the curb. "There's my driver now."

Nick took her elbow. Just as he'd thought, he mused, looking at the car. Rich. "It's occurred to me I don't even know your name," he drawled as a beefy Latin driver got out and held the door for them.

"Robyn," she said. Picking up her skirts in both hands, she spoke to the driver in a voice that seemed heavy with meaning. "Mr. Wyatt will be joining us, Joseito."

"Yes, ma'am," Joseito replied.

Nick slipped in beside her, enjoying the flash of trim ankle he saw before her skirts slid back down into place. "Robyn what?" he asked. Although they'd just met, already his blood was sizzling in his veins. The car left the curb with a purr.

"Are names really that important to you, Nick?" She bent forward and opened the bar. Glancing at the collection of bottles, she braced herself against the forward motion of the car and said, "Would you like some champagne?"

Why not? Nick thought. Considering the night he had ahead of him, he deserved the chance to relax, if only for a little while. He looked out at the city streets, appreciating their driver's smooth steady pace. "Please. So where are we going?" he asked while Robyn poured.

Their hands touched as she handed him the tulip-shaped glass. Nick's heart accelerated a little more as she leaned back in her seat and poured herself some champagne. Again she sent him a flirtatious glance. Now here, Nick thought, was a woman who could incite a war.

"Where would you like to go?" she asked softly as the car paused at a stoplight.

Nick sipped his champagne. The interior of the car was filled with the scent of her perfume, and the equally compelling, equally feminine fragrance of her hair and skin. He wanted to be closer, but because she had chosen to sit facing him, he remained where he was and simply enjoyed the view, even as he delivered the bad news. "Where I would like to go and where I can go are two different things, unfortunately," he said, not bothering to mask the depth of his regret, or his wish to spend time with her. "I have a meeting later this evening."

Robyn pouted prettily, as he'd half hoped she would. "Can't you put it off? I really have a yen to see the gulf."

"Now?" Nick asked dryly as the limo began moving once again. "Tonight?"

Robyn shrugged and released the button closure of her cloak. The rich velvet slid across her shoulders. Nick's glance moved to the sexiness of her bare shoulders and well-defined upper arms before traveling to the diamond heart on a gold chain that dangled in her shadowy décolletage. Her breasts were high and full, the creamy globes spilling out above the vee neck of her figure-hugging beaded evening gown.

"Why not?" Robyn persisted as the limo picked up speed. "It's only a few hours away, by plane."

It was all Nick could do not to groan out loud. "As delightful as that sounds, I'm afraid I can't, Robyn. Not tonight."

"Is this meeting you have business or pleasure?" she queried lightly.

What Nick thought she really wanted to know was if there was another woman involved. If there had been, she would have been history the first time Robyn smiled at him. "Business," he said shortly.

She smiled, crossed her legs and turned slightly, revealing a thigh-high slit in the left side of the gown that sent his pulse skyrocketing. "That's too bad." Still smiling sexily, she looked at him over the rim of her glass.

Nick tore his eyes from the slim lines of her leg, the long slender thigh, the cute knee, the shapely calf and trim ankle above a delicately small foot. All were encased in silky sheer white stocking adorned with fleursde-lis. And those heels...the sexy three-inch heels were made to make the most of a woman's legs.

Nick let out a slow, controlled breath. He wasn't in the habit of picking up women, but if he had been, he wouldn't have hesitated now. Unfortunately, duty called and he had put off his obligation to the family business far too long as it was. "Maybe some other time," he said, meaning it.

Robyn fell silent, her disappointment in his decision evident. Struggling with a few regrets of his own, Nick glanced out the tinted windows again. He was surprised to see they'd merged onto the freeway without him ever realizing it and were easily keeping pace with the swift, steady flow of evening traffic.

Robyn's fingers clasped the stem of her glass more tightly. "Suppose I told you there couldn't be another time?" she retorted coyly, looking more determined than ever to have her own way. And yet, Nick thought, she didn't seem spoiled, at least in the way the rich young heiresses he met usually were.

"Then I'd be very sorry," he said softly, wondering why tonight was so very important to the mysterious beauty. And where was she taking him? he wondered, looking out the window once again. They appeared to be headed west.

Robyn studied his expression carefully. "I can't change your mind?"

Nick shook his head. "Sorry. I've got an hour though," Nick said, thinking maybe they could go somewhere nice and get better acquainted.

Robyn frowned her dissatisfaction with his counteroffer. "I'm afraid that's not long enough," she said firmly before he could ask her to have dinner with him.

Not long enough for what? Nick felt both flattered and amused by her unexpectedly persistent attitude. "We could be together tomorrow evening. All evening."

To his surprise, Robyn looked even more displeased with his softly voiced proposal. "That won't work, either. I'll be in Mexico. In fact, there's a jet at Alliance airport waiting to take me to my villa right now."

Nick was even more intrigued. If Robyn was flying out of Alliance, that meant she was flying on either a corporate or private chartered jet. "When will you be back?" he asked.

She shrugged. "A week or so." She smiled at him seductively. "Sure I can't talk you into it?" she asked softly, her brown eyes both earnest and intent.

Nick was tempted. He was sorely tempted. He hadn't ever met a woman who affected him so. "No. In fact—" he glanced at his watch, then the freeway signs, which said they were already in Fort Worth "—you'd better stop the car and let me hail a cab. I've really got to get back to Dallas."

She sighed and put her glass down. Reaching for the telephone, she picked it up and spoke to the driver. "Joseito, Mr. Wyatt does not want to go with us. In fact, he'd like to get out of the car as soon as possible." She smiled, as if at some private joke, then sighed softly, as with great regret. "I know." She frowned. "Me, too."

Call it gut feeling, call it intuition, Nick suddenly had a very funny feeling. "What's going on?" he asked. Without warning the back door locks clicked and the limo continued to speed along I-35 West.

Robyn sat back against the seat and smiled at him. "What makes you think something is going on?" she asked in her soft, smoky voice.

The car sped past an exit without so much as an attempt to stop.

Nick didn't know what Robyn was up to, but he wasn't about to be shanghaied, not even by a very persistent, very beautiful woman. "Okay. This is where I get out," he said heavily, his expression grim. "Tell Joseito to take the next exit and let me off somewhere I can call a cab."

Robyn leaned forward to put her glass aside, involuntarily treating him to a better view of her cleavage. She slowly sat back in her seat. The only sign of her nervousness was the tight way she was gripping her beaded evening bag. Her eyes on his, she said steadily, in a way that let him know her earlier come-on had been just a way to manipulate him, "I can't do that, Nick."

"What do you mean you can't do that?" Nick demanded. He was beginning to get angry.

"I have orders—"

"Orders!" he interrupted, his jaw tightening ferociously. "From whom?"

Robyn increased her death grip on the purse in her lap and regarded him steadily, all business now. "I can't tell you that, either." Perspiration broke out on her upper lip as she slipped her tongue out to wet her lower lip.

Suddenly, everything fell into place. "Leland's behind this, isn't he?" Nick asked, then swore vituperatively, knowing it was true even if Robyn wouldn't confirm it. His fists clenched and he pounded his thighs. "I knew my mother never should have married him!"

Robyn swallowed hard. "Leland Kincaid is a good man," she disagreed.

Nick's glance shot up. He pinned her with a probing look. "You're in cahoots with him?"

Again, to his fury, she said nothing. The limo left the freeway and sped across concrete to a private hangar, where a small jet waited. "You can't get away with this," Nick said, already sizing up the burly driver behind the glass, and the treacherously beautiful woman across from him—whom he knew he could take in less time than she could blink.

"Oh, I'm afraid I not only can, I will, Nick." She reached into her purse and withdrew a small caliber, very lethal looking gun. "Like you," she said heavily, "I have no choice."

Chapter Two

"This is insane!" Nick said, gaping at her.

"Please stay calm, Nick," Robyn advised in the steadiest voice she could manage, hoping she looked more menacing than she felt. "No one wants you to be hurt."

Nick Wyatt's mouth compressed into a tight white line. All the laughter left his dark pine green eyes. "That's a funny thing to be saying when you're holding a gun on me," he growled.

"If you'd just cooperated," Robyn defended herself hotly, "it wouldn't have been necessary to use a gun at all."

"Meaning what? You could have lured me there and I never would have been any the wiser?"

Robyn flushed. "Something like that."

A muscle worked in Nick's jaw as he glanced at the gun she clutched firmly in both hands, and then back at her face. She could tell by the intent, analytical way he looked at her that he was weighing his options, biding his time. She didn't like the idea of getting into a physical tussle with him; something told her, gun or no, she would lose. No matter how much she wished otherwise.

Fortunately for her, before Nick could make a move, the limo halted. The hangar doors slid shut via remote. Their mingled breaths sounding loudly in the hushed interior of the car, she and Nick continued their wary staring match.

"Look," he said finally with a gruff sigh. He held every inch of his rugged six-two frame absolutely motionless, respectful of the gun yet somehow braced for battle just the same. "It's obvious you've made a mistake here. I'm not thrilled about it, but I'm willing to put my unhappiness with this whole stupid, crazy episode aside," Nick said with grudging generosity. His eyes focused on hers with the intensity of twin lasers. *"Providing it ends now, Robyn."*

"Forget it, Nick," Robyn said briskly as she heard Joseito get out of the driver's seat and shut the door. The heavy man's footsteps sounded on the concrete floor of the hangar, reassuring and threatening all at once. "You can't talk your way out of this." *Just as I can't get out of it, either, no matter how much a part of me now wants to.*

"Come on, Robyn," Nick persuaded softly, hurriedly, aware time was running out for both of them as Joseito yanked open the door.

The bulky man's shadow fell over them, but Nick's attention was focused solely on Robyn as his eyes swiftly searched her face. "You and I both know you don't really want to do this," Nick continued. "You're not cut out for the criminal life-style. Let me go now and I swear I'll never say anything to anyone, about either of you. I promise.''

Robyn struggled with her own conflictive feelings about the kidnapping, then thought, just as swiftly, of the picture of Nick she'd seen plastered on the front page of the *Naughty Not Nice* supermarket tabloid. He had been reclining in a huge king-size bed. A sheet had been drawn up over his most private parts, but it was easy to see from the exposed length of one very sexy hip and thigh that he was naked underneath.

He'd been surrounded by four scantily clad women. Two blondes, a brunette and a redhead had all been touching, kissing and caressing Nick in some way while Nick, darn every hedonistic playboy inch of him, lay back with a sublime, almost dopey expression of pleasure on his far-too-handsome-for-his-own-good face. How much more of a reminder did she need to realize that Nick was not concerned with family business?

Nick Wyatt was a pleasure seeker extraordinaire who didn't care a whit about either his mother's feelings or the family business. Otherwise, he wouldn't have done even half the things he'd done lately. Appealing to his conscience was not likely to have any effect at all on him. And she knew she couldn't trust him to do the right thing even if she told him everything, right this minute. Whether she liked it or not, she was left no choice.

Robyn drew a deep bolstering breath and retorted with the same steely determination that had propelled her career to the top, "If I let you go now, Nick, Joseito and I will be in jail before midnight."

Nick's mouth tightened. He shook his head in mute remonstrance. "You think I'll feel more kindly toward you after a week passes?" he asked sarcastically.

"I don't know." Robyn resisted the urge to wipe her hands, which were slippery with sweat, on her velvet cloak, instead keeping them tightly clenched around the handle of the gun. "Maybe not," she allowed stonily.

The corners of Nick's mouth lifted. "Then why kidnap me?" he asked softly, sexily.

Because my whole future, the achievement of a lifelong dream, depends upon it. "Because I have to," she said firmly as her hand trembled.

She could tell by the way he was looking at her that Nick was still thinking about rushing her, but was also worried about what would happen if the gun went off while they tussled. Would Joseito shoot him? He, too, had a gun. And he looked infinitely more comfortable with his than she did with hers, Robyn realized with relief.

"Mr. Wyatt, we have wasted enough time with this idle chitchat. Put your hands up above your head and step slowly out of the car, if you please," Joseito said in his heavily accented voice. His black eyes utterly humorless, he watched as Nick complied. "Thank you." He nodded his head in the direction of the small sleek jet. "Now walk slowly to the plane."

"Look, if it's money you want," Nick said in a bored voice, over his shoulder as he swaggered lazily toward the private jet, "I'll help you arrange for a ransom."

Robyn blew out a short breath, irked that Nick would think they were so greedy and simpleminded, and focused instead on the rumpled, long layers of his ash brown hair. She emerged from the car still holding the gun on Nick and grabbed her coat and evening purse with her left hand. "If it's money we wanted," she retorted dryly, "all we'd have to do is arrange to photograph some more of your exploits."

His steps slowing somewhat, Nick turned to look at her over his shoulder. As she gazed at him, Robyn thought she had never seen a man look so James Bond-ish good in a simple black tux and pleated white shirt. He knew it, too. He probably counted on his looks to get him whatever he wanted.

Nick's probing glance narrowed suspiciously. "So you were behind that," he surmised grimly.

Robyn blinked. "Behind what?" she asked, confused as she continued to keep to Joseito's left and back, so she could see Nick and talk to him and yet have the protection of Joseito between them.

"Those four girls!" Nick said, glancing back at her again.

"I assume you're talking about your latest 'photo opportunity'?" Robyn asked sarcastically.

Nick turned all the way around. The grim set of his mouth matched the grimness in his eyes. "What else?"

His raking glance left her feeling both naked and aroused. "Listen, Nick Wyatt, I may be a lot of things," she countered stonily, embarrassed by her immediate physical response to the man, "but I am not a handler for race-car-driver groupies." Nor was she the criminal he deemed her to be.

"So what do you do, besides kidnap people?" Nick prodded, his expression deadpan.

Sensing things were getting too hot between Robyn and Nick, the oft-silent Joseito put his burly frame squarely between them and intervened. "On the plane, Mr. Wyatt, if you please." Joseito followed Nick up to the passenger area, where there was a single bath, a sofa that could also be used for sleeping along one side of the plane, and two chairs with a collapsible table in between. Joseito motioned to the two chairs that faced each other, and directed Nick into the one farthest from the cockpit. "In that seat."

Nick complied recalcitrantly. Only, Robyn thought, because he had no choice. She also knew Nick's calm was deceptive. Sooner or later he would make his move, and there would be hell to pay for all of them when he did.

Forcing her mind back to her duties, she removed twin sets of silver handcuffs from her evening bag and, with Joseito looking on gruffly, knelt reluctantly to handcuff Nick to the seat, one wrist to each armrest.

When he was secured, Joseito closed the door and retired to the cockpit. Robyn sat opposite Nick. He looked mad enough to spit and she couldn't really blame him. In his place, she'd be resentful as hell, and frightened, too.

Nick was silent as the plane took off. When they were airborne, he picked up as if they had never stopped talking. "If it's not money you want," he asked point-blank, "then why did you kidnap me?"

"*Kidnap*'s such a harsh word." Robyn put her handbag, with the gun inside, well out of reach, then resumed her seat.

"But appropriate," Nick disagreed as he struggled without much success to get more comfortable.

"Why not look at this as an extended vacation?" Robyn asked lightly. She was going to do everything within her power to make his unexpected stay with them as pleasant as possible. "I am," she said confidently, sure that once Nick accepted the situation for what it was, and realized he may as well grin and bear it, that they would be fine.

"Taking a vacation means willfully going away," Nick countered, his temper showing. His glance veered deliberately to the plunging neckline of her dress before returning with aggravating slowness to her face. "I'm not."

Wishing she could stop tingling everywhere his eyes had touched, she gave him a level glance. "Sometimes it's necessary to do something even if you don't initially want to." For instance, she wasn't pleased about what she was doing here tonight, but she had been convinced it was very necessary, not just for her welfare, but the welfare of countless others. Knowing those people depended on her strengthened her conviction that although her actions were unusual, they weren't wrong.

"I see," Nick said slowly, with biting sarcasm. "My being kidnapped is sort of like taking medicine."

"Sort of," Robyn agreed.

"Only I'm not sick," Nick pointed out as his glance roved her lips.

"No," Robyn volleyed back without thinking, wishing his chest didn't look so strong and solid beneath the starched white fabric of his shirt, "but you are a nuisance."

He gave her a sexy half smile and sat as far back in his seat as the handcuffs would allow. "How do you know I'm a nuisance?"

Her chin shot up and she regarded him smugly. "Because I heard all about the way you treated your mother after her recent remarriage. Like a pariah, and not a particularly bright one at that. Honestly, Nick, don't you think your mother has a right to be happy again? To choose her own mate?"

"You're telling me my mother's behind this? Or is it Leland?" Nick asked.

"Joseito and I are doing what's best for Wyatt & Company, yes," Robyn replied evasively. Even if it sounded crazy, it was the absolute truth.

Nick's expression grew even grimmer. The set of his broad shoulders became even more imposing. "Spiriting me away is not what's best for Wyatt & Company, believe me."

Feeling increasingly restless, Robyn got up to prowl the small interior of the jet. "I hardly think you're in a position to know." She looked out the opposite bay of windows and saw only the blackness of night below them.

"What's that supposed to mean?"

Robyn whirled to face him. She clamped her arms defiantly beneath her breasts. "It means you've never once shown any interest in your family company."

Nick rolled his eyes and used his feet to swivel the seat of his chair around on the base, so that he was facing her. "Like I'm supposed to be interested in women's clothing."

Robyn paced restlessly back and forth. "It's a business, Nick."

He laughed derisively. "A fashion rip-off is more like it. The major designers change the look every year so women will have to buy a whole new wardrobe or look hopelessly out-of-date. Like I said," he added when she opened her mouth to disagree, "a rip-off."

Robyn inclined her head and gave him a dissecting look. "And what would you have women do, Nick?" she asked sweetly. "Look the same year after year?"

He shrugged as if that were exactly what he would do. "Works for us men."

"Well, it wouldn't work for me or the majority of women I know." Robyn tossed her head and drove her fingers through the hair at her temples, pushing the thick silky waves off her face. "I'd get bored with the same look."

Silence fell between them once again, even more uncomfortable now. Nick shifted, testing the handcuff and sturdiness of the chair. "So how do you know my stepfather?'' Nick probed, all but ignoring her watchful presence as he attempted to physically negotiate his release. ''You his latest girlfriend, or what?''

Robyn knew he was baiting her deliberately, trying to get more information out of her, but his accusations were so far off the mark she shot back emphatically, ''Leland does not have any women on the side, Nick.'' Leland was devoted to his new wife, Nick's mother, Cassandra.

Nick narrowed his eyes disbelievingly. ''Sure about that?'' he asked silkily.

Realizing she had already said far too much, Robyn said calmly, ''Can we change the subject, please?''

''Not until I know how you're linked to Leland. You work for him?''

''Why does it matter?''

He chafed against the cuffs, his frustration mounting. ''I want to know who I'm dealing with.''

Robyn shrugged. Knowing he would find out this much eventually anyway, she said, ''Consider me a friend of the family.''

He raised an imperious brow. ''Friends of the family don't handcuff said family to the chair.'' He paused. ''I could have you prosecuted for this, you know''

Robyn shrugged. ''We're way ahead of you there, Nick. Leland will testify it was merely an extravagant practical joke, within the family. So will your mother, if it comes to that.''

"My mother's in on this, too?" Nick asked, not bothering to hide his shock or his dismay.

"Of course," Robyn said. At least Leland had said Cassandra was. He'd said she wanted Nick out of Dallas until the latest brouhaha over his picture in *Naughty Not Nice* had died down. Looking at Nick's disbelieving expression, though, she had to wonder. Then she pushed her doubts aside. She had no reason to doubt anything Leland said, but plenty of reason to doubt Nick.

Nick released a lengthy sigh. "Damn," he said. He shook his head and closed his eyes in defeat.

Robyn knew just how he felt.

NICK COULDN'T BELIEVE his mother was in on this, too, but then she had changed since his father's death. Become someone he hardly knew.

"Are you hungry?" Robyn asked solicitously.

He was about to say no when he realized this could be his ticket out of here. "Famished. What do you have?"

Robyn disappeared into the small gallery between the cockpit and the seats and returned with a tray full of sandwiches, fruit and sodas. She set the tray down on the collapsible table between them and served him with the same polite, remote efficiency as a stewardess in first class. "What would you like? Ham or chicken?"

Like I really care at this point, Nick thought, but he kept his voice sufficiently subdued as he answered, "Ham."

Robyn started to hand the sandwich to him, then paused, biting her lip. He looked longingly at the food. "The handcuffs are going to have to go," Nick said. "Unless—" he shot her a hopeful glance rife with innuendo "—you want to feed me bite by bite by luscious bite?"

Robyn ignored his thinly veiled pass. Appearing all the more beautiful and distressed, she said, "I can't free you, Nick. Not while we're in the air." She glanced away, refusing to look at him directly. "It's too dangerous."

Provoked into mischievousness, Nick asked softly, "What do you think I'm going to do?"

Her spine stiffened, the action thrusting her breasts out even more above the beaded plunging neckline of her dress. Nick felt his mouth go dry and his lower body tighten.

"I don't know," Robyn said, looking into his eyes, then hastily away, "and I don't want to find out."

"Come on. I'll behave," Nick persuaded. "I promise." He paused, waiting until she glanced at him again before he continued, "Now that I know it's all in the way of family high jinks and that you're not really out to hurt me, you're right, why should I fight? Why not just kick back and relax on an expense-paid vacation with a beautiful babe? And you are beautiful, sweetheart. Very beautiful," he finished honestly. *Even if you do have a treacherous heart.*

Robyn hesitated, looking as if restraining him that way really went against the grain with her. She bit her lip. "Will you promise to behave?" she asked.

He nodded.

Swallowing, she slid the key into the left handcuff and released it. Still holding her gaze, he slipped his hand out, captured her wrist and pulled her onto his lap. Ignoring her gasp of dismay, he grasped one of her wrists and pinned the other between them. Just that fast, she was trapped on his lap.

Color streamed into her cheeks. Her sable eyes were wide, distressed. "You said you wouldn't try anything," Robyn said, her bottom scooting across his lap as she initially went limp with shock, then immediately struggled like a wild thing to be free.

Nick's lips curved in a parody of a smile. "I lied."

"Let me go."

Feeling as if he'd need a fire hose to put out the flames in his groin if she didn't stop wiggling immediately, he increased the pressure on her chest. Breathless, she slumped against his chest and stared up at him. "I'll pay you double what Leland is giving you," Nick offered. Everyone—even this beautiful angel with a black heart—had a price. He only had to find it to be free.

Robyn angled her head as far back as it could go, until it rested against his shoulder. "He's not paying me," she said hotly as her chest heaved.

The fabric of her dress was thin. Nick felt the increasing heat of her skin and the tightening bud of one of her nipples against his forearm. "Now why do I find that hard to believe?" he taunted, trying not to notice how soft her skin was, how fragrant she smelled.

"Because it's true!" Robyn pushed against his restraining arm with her hand, then went pale.

"Now who's stretching the truth?" Nick asked impatiently. He hadn't liked being kidnapped. He really hated being lied to, especially after the jig was up. "The man's a snake, Robyn," he continued.

"Isn't that a little like the pot calling the kettle black?"

"What do you mean?"

"I mean," Robyn sputtered with annoyance, "your romantic exploits are legendary."

Nick was so tired of people judging him by what they read in tabloid trash like *Naughty Not Nice*. He expelled a long breath. "If you're talking about the fact I like to race cars, fly jets and mountain climb—"

"I'm talking about your exploits with women."

Nick rolled his eyes. That again. "The rumors of my exploits are greatly exaggerated."

The resentment in her eyes faded and she regarded him cautiously. "What do you call the article in *Naughty Not Nice* then?"

"Leland's handiwork," Nick said heavily, not even trying to suppress his anger. "He's trying to make me look bad to my mother. If you'd just let me explain everything that's been going on, I'm sure we can straighten all this out."

Robyn stopped struggling altogether and gave him a bored, almost impatient look. "Leland said you would say anything to get me on your side, Nick, but grabbing me like this is not going to make me listen to you.''

She looked so judgmental. ''Is there any way to make you listen to me?'' Nick demanded, his own temper beginning to soar.

''Not really, no!'' Robyn volleyed back, just as rudely. She looked at him stubbornly from beneath the fringe of thick dark lashes. ''I prefer to stick to the facts. And the fact of the matter is that, like it or not, you were caught in bed with four scantily dressed women!''

''I'm not denying that,'' Nick said, exasperated. ''Obviously, I was there,'' he explained.

''And obviously, you were naked. Even if the women weren't . . . quite—''

''But I was set up,'' Nick continued stonily.

Her expression changed abruptly and she shoved against him. ''Leland told me you would say that, too, Nick. But I saw the picture. I saw the way those women were kissing and caressing you simultaneously. I saw the dopey, almost sublime expression on your face! You were enjoying every hedonistic moment of it! Why can't you just be a man about it and own up to that? You wanted to go to bed with four women, to celebrate your victory, and you did. But this time, you got caught!''

He grabbed her before she could get all the way off his lap, and pulled her back. Even with only one arm, his grip was absolutely unshakable. ''Will you just hear me out, dammit? The last thing I recall is winning the race at Daytona,'' Nick continued. ''I know

I was picked up by a limo. I was supposed to go to a party afterward." Nick frowned as his memories turned fuzzy. "But I never got to the party. They must've put something in my Gatorade. I remember I thought it tasted a little funny, but I was really thirsty, so I drank it quickly anyway."

She gave him a deadpan look. "If you expect me or anyone else to buy the somebody-put-something-in-my-drink story you're really an idiot."

"It's the truth," Nick defended himself hotly. "I had blood tests taken that prove I was drugged!"

"Right."

"If you will just let me go and or take me back to Dallas, I can prove it, dammit. I've got copies of those tests in the glove compartment of my car," Nick insisted.

"Yeah, right, Nick, I'm sure you do." Robyn shook her head in mute disbelief. "You just won't quit with the tall tales, will you?"

"You're damn right I'm not going to quit," Nick volleyed back. He was furious she wouldn't listen to him, frustrated beyond belief at being first shanghaied, then confined this way. It was so unfair, and looking into her face, he saw that she knew not only that, but that his patience, what very little had been left of it, had come to an end.

Her expression panicked, she started to call out for help. "Oh, God. Jo—"

She got no further than the first sound of her hired henchman's name when Nick silenced her with a quick, hard kiss. He'd meant just to shut her up, to keep her from yelling out for her buddy, until he could get his hand over her mouth to suppress the cry for help, but something happened when their lips touched. Hers softened beneath his. Right away. She sucked in a quick urgent breath. He felt her shock in the stiffness of her limbs, in the unresponsiveness of her soft mouth. Suddenly he knew, as with any challenge, that he could get past it.

She clamped her lips shut. He slid his tongue along the seam. She perched more stiffly. He became more persistent. Who knew what would have happened if the jet hadn't landed while they were locked in each other's arms? But it had, Nick realized with shock as the jet bumped and bounced when the wheels hit the tarmac.

The second's inattentiveness was all Robyn needed. With a quick elbow to his ribs, she was up and off his lap, backing away. Her hair all tousled, her lips damp and swollen from the kiss, her eyes glittering with suppressed desire, she looked even lovelier than she had at the symphony.

"Don't you ever...*ever*...do that again."

"Sure?" he taunted lazily, silently cursing himself for allowing himself to be sidetracked by his desire for her instead of using the opportunity to get the handcuff key so he could free himself. "You really seemed to enjoy it."

Her eyes blazed as she swept her hands through her hair, restoring order as best she could. "Well, I didn't!"

He looked at her heaving chest, at the way her nipples were distended beneath the fabric of her dress, and taunted her again, very softly. "Liar."

The jet rolled to a stop. Nick looked out the window and saw nothing but a few runway lights. His despair mounted as he realized they had landed on a private airstrip.

"Well, well," he remarked drolly, as Robyn moved to reclaim her gun. "Looks like we're here."

Chapter Three

"Has he been giving you trouble, Robyn?" Joseito asked. He stepped through the cockpit door, shiny black revolver in hand.

Trouble? Was a steamy, sensual kiss she'd felt all the way down to her toes trouble? Or was it more like magic, Robyn's romantic nature prodded. The kind she had read about but never before experienced.

Joseito gave her an inquiring look as he picked up the extra set of handcuffs and tossed them to her.

"Nothing I can't handle," Robyn lied as she moved around behind Nick. Leland had been right. Nick was lethal when it came to getting his own way. She was glad she didn't have to handle him alone any longer. Glad he wouldn't have another chance to kiss her.

"It's not my intention to hurt her or you," Nick reassured the stone-faced man as Joseito planted a beefy hand on Nick's shoulder and pushed him forward in the chair. Knowing it imperative they do a better job of subduing Nick on the journey ahead of them, Robyn jerked Nick's arms behind him and manacled his hands together before releasing the lock on the handcuff that still held him to the chair. Aware that her hands were shaking, her knees unsteady, she quickly backed away.

Joseito grunted at Nick and gestured with the gun, indicating he wanted Nick to stand.

With a beleaguered smirk, Nick got slowly to his feet and sauntered to the exit as if he were trouble-free. He started down the handful of steps to the tarmac below, where a sleek black car waited. He yawned hugely. "Another limo?"

"We want you to be as comfortable as possible," Robyn reassured sincerely as she gathered up her belongings and followed the men out of the jet and onto the deserted runway.

"I'll just bet you do," Nick said heavily. He raked Robyn with a scorching glance. "Tell me, sweetheart, is there a bed and four naked women where we're going?"

"You wish," Robyn snapped, her cheeks burning as she thought about the photo of Nick and those women that had appeared in the previous week's issue of *Naughty Not Nice*. She could still recall the flatness of his abdomen, the wealth of suntanned skin and the absence of any swimsuit line. Which had to mean he sunbathed sans swimsuit, with every glorious six-foot-two inch of him exposed to the sun—and whoever might be wandering by.

His hands in cuffs behind him, Nick got into the car. Robyn followed. Joseito waited until he was sure they were settled before going around to the front and slipping behind the wheel.

As Joseito drove, Nick looked out the window and contemplated his options. It was clear from the road signs that they were in Mexico. A pilot himself, he judged from the time the flight had taken—a little under two hours—that they were at least one hundred miles across the border. Great, he thought. Not only was he faced with the prospect of trying to escape, he also had to figure out what to do if and when he did manage to ditch the two nitwits holding him hostage.

Mexico wasn't like the United States. Even a simple traffic violation here could mean a long stay in jail. Sure, he could go to the Mexican police and swear he'd been kidnapped. But then they'd have to hold him until he had proven beyond a reasonable doubt that he had indeed been kidnapped. By that time, Robyn and Joseito would be long gone. He could try to bribe the police, of course, but he sensed the two hundred American dollars he had on him wouldn't go very far, in either bribes or travel arrangements. And he doubted very much they'd be willing to take American Express.

No, whatever happened, Nick reasoned, he would have to manage on his wits alone. And he couldn't count on anyone to help. Not even the very beautiful, very sensuous, very responsive Robyn, for it was clear she had been hoodwinked just like his mother. He frowned. It was hard to know what lies Leland had told Robyn about him to get her to cooperate, or what he had promised as her reward, but it was clear she felt she was doing something noble in getting him out of the country.

Without warning, they approached a small Mexican village. There were blazing lights and an abundance of loud mariachi music. "What's going on up ahead?"

As they drove around the cordoned-off plaza, Robyn noted with excitement, "It looks like some sort of festival."

That was obvious, Nick thought as he looked out the dark glass windows of the limo to the brightly clad people dancing in the streets. Young, old, everyone seemed to be having a great time.

"Oh, I love to dance." Robyn sighed, settling back in her seat. "I wish I could join them."

"You'd be just a little conspicuous in that gown, don't you think?" Nick drawled, seeing no reason to try to be pleasant, considering the way he'd been shanghaied.

"Guess you're right. I do need clothes." Robyn smiled at Nick like a kid embarking on her very first adventure, then picked up the car phone and demanded crisply, "Joseito, how much farther to the villa?"

Nick stretched his long legs out in front of him. Having his arms clamped behind him this way was damned uncomfortable. And it was made more so because a certain part of his anatomy was still aching in a way it hadn't since he'd been a teenage kid.

Robyn opened the cabinet and began fiddling with the television set. She couldn't pick up much of anything, the reception was so bad, and finally she inserted a tape in the VCR instead. Delighted, she sat back to watch Goldie Hawn and Chevy Chase spar in *Seems Like Old Times*.

Peeved that she could actually sit and watch a movie at a time like this, Nick accused, "You're actually having fun!"

"Of course," Robyn admitted with an unabashed smile. "I've never been to Mexico. Never been outside the continental U.S."

So she wasn't rich, Nick thought grimly. Was money, or want of it, what was really motivating her? Somehow, he hadn't figured her for the greedy type.

Robyn rummaged around the cabinet, pulled out a package of cigars and a bottle of aged brandy. "Darn. I was hoping for some popcorn," she said. Then laughed, delighted. "After all, there's a tiny microwave here to cook it! Can you imagine that! Having your own microwave in your car?"

Nick scowled. Having grown up riding in limousines with every convenience imaginable, the contents of the cabinet were no big deal to him. "Why haven't you ever been outside the United States?"

Robyn glanced over her shoulder at him and sat back in her seat. Using the remote control, she stopped the movie in play and hit the mute button. "Not everyone is born with a silver spoon in his—or her— mouth, Nick."

"Where were you born?" Nick asked. Who was she? And why hadn't he seen her before? Did she really know his mother, or was that a lie? He couldn't see her as criminal. Misguided, hopelessly naive and easily led, yes, but criminal? No, she didn't have that hard ruthless immoral edge necessary to commit crimes. And yet, he thought, she had helped shanghai him to parts unknown.

"Umm, I'm from East Texas. Why?" Robyn went back to rummaging around in the cabinet and finally came up with a package of peanuts. She offered him some. He refused. She tore open the package and munched contentedly.

"We may as well do something to pass the time. Since I can't kiss you again—"

"Very funny." Robyn popped a few more peanuts in her mouth.

"—I figured we may as well talk. So," he continued without giving her a chance to interrupt, "what brought you to Dallas?"

"Specifically? The Apparel Mart at Dallas Market Center. I love clothes."

She certainly wore them well enough, Nick thought. "Enough to work for Wyatt & Company?" he asked.

Robyn sobered abruptly. "It's a good company, Nick."

Nick studied her earnest expression. She really believed in what she was doing. And yet she didn't seem like a nut case. Or even, he thought, like someone who could be bought. "So how long have you been with them?" he asked.

"Twelve years. I worked there summers while I was in college. After I graduated, I moved to Dallas and took a full-time position with Wyatt & Co."

"What area are you in?" he asked.

Robyn finished her bag of peanuts and crumpled the empty silver sack into a ball. She aimed for the tiny trash container in the cabinet and hit it perfectly. "Design."

"Like it?"

She grinned and rummaged through the small refrigerator. "I love it." She finally emerged empty-handed. "Darn. I would kill for a Coke. I am so thirsty."

As it happened, so was Nick. He regarded her casually. "None in there, hmm?"

She shook her head with obvious regret. "Only Mexican beer."

"Don't like it?"

"Don't know. I haven't tried it."

"Go ahead," he urged. Having her even the slightest bit tipsy could only work to his advantage.

"I don't think so," she said firmly.

"Why not?"

"I don't want to dull my reflexes."

Remembering the way she had kissed him back, even when she hadn't wanted to, Nick didn't want that, either. He could only speculate what it might be like to have her fully cooperative, and in his bed. To hear her soft, ecstatic cries...

"Oh, look," Robyn said as Joseito made a sharp left turn into a long, winding driveway. "We're here," Robyn said with obvious excitement.

Nick yawned and spared her a cynical glance. "I can't wait."

"CAN YOU BELIEVE this place?" Robyn gushed minutes later as the three of them sauntered up the walk from the detached garage to the white stone villa on the bluff high above the ocean. Below them was a beach, and in the distance, rolling hills, lots of trees, and the beginnings of mountainous terrain. Nick could detect no other buildings except the spire of a church that rose high above the trees. "It's beautiful," she said.

Robyn waited for Joseito to unlock the door, then pranced inside. "I've never seen so many beautiful rooms. It'll take hours to explore this place," she enthused.

The sprawling three-story villa was like countless others Nick had been in. "A few minutes, tops," he disagreed.

Robyn whirled on him, hands on her slender hips. "Don't be such a party pooper!" she chided.

"Can't help it." He yawned, putting on a show of fatigue. "I've already seen as much as I want to see." He feigned the malleableness of a newborn kitten. "Just lead me to my prison and let me be."

To his surprise, Robyn looked disappointed and a little hurt by his lack of enthusiasm. "Very well," she said crisply, looping her evening cloak over a chair. "We'll put you in your room."

The three of them headed up one flight of stairs, and then another. "So what's next?" Nick drawled in an unimpressed tone. "Going to handcuff me to the bed?"

Robyn bristled at even the hint they'd been mistreating him. "Don't be silly. We'll just lock you in, won't we, Joseito?"

Joseito nodded silently.

Nick didn't want to be locked in a room alone. He wanted to be locked in a room with Robyn. But there wasn't much of a chance of that, with her giant bodyguard around. "Not much of a talker, are you, Joseito?" Nick baited, wishing the guy wasn't so big. Nick was strong—and smart enough to know he couldn't fight someone who had six inches and seventy pounds on him. Especially when the other guy had a gun in his hand. No, he'd have to get out of this on wits alone.

They led him down a long corridor. Robyn strolled the lavishly appointed bedroom and peeked inside the adjacent bath. "You've got everything you need here, Nick," she reported, pleased.

Nick wished she would quit acting like a social director on a cruise ship. "Except a phone."

He expected a smart remark from her. Instead, she sobered unexpectedly and said softly, honestly, "I'm sorry it had to be this way, Nick."

"Does it?" he asked lightly, the idea of seducing her into helping him becoming infinitely more palatable now that he knew for certain that this kidnapping wasn't really her cup of tea.

"Robyn," Joseito interrupted.

"The giant speaks," Nick drawled.

"You know what Mr. Kincaid said," Joseito reminded Robyn, then turned to Nick. "We have strict instructions not to let you manipulate us into helping you. Mr. Kincaid said you would try.''

''I'll just bet he did,'' Nick muttered between his teeth as Robyn unlocked the handcuffs and removed them. She stared up into his eyes, and for the briefest of seconds, he could have sworn she wanted nothing more than to release him.

''Come along, Robyn. Nick has everything he needs.''

''Except my freedom,'' Nick added bitterly.

To his disappointment, Robyn had no reply for that. Regret in her eyes, she left, with Joseito on her heels.

RUBBING THE PLACES on his wrists where the handcuffs had been, Nick cased his room. The hall door was bolted shut from the outside, so there was only one way out, and that was by the French doors that led to the third-floor balcony outside. Once his escape plan had been formulated, Nick didn't waste any time making preparations. He removed the sheets from his bed and began tearing them into strips, then worked quickly and quietly to fashion a long, sturdy rope. By dawn, he was rappeling down the side of the villa.

Seeing Robyn sound asleep in the bedroom located just beneath his, her revolver on the nightstand beside her bed, gave Nick pause, but he forced himself to keep going. He could use the gun to aid his escape, but if he tried to get it he might wake her. If she screamed, Joseito would probably come running, his own gun in hand. Nick didn't think the burly henchman actually wanted to shoot him, but who knew what might happen in the confusion, particularly if the protective Joseito thought Nick was hurting Robyn. No, it wasn't worth the risk, he decided as he continued rappeling down the side of the house.

Besides, with any luck it would be hours before Joseito even realized he was missing. By the time he did, Nick reasoned, he would be long gone anyway. All he had to do was get the hell out of here, hike to the closest American embassy, get a tourist card, and he'd be on his way home, where he could deal with that SOB of a stepfather in person.

The garage was empty save for the black limousine they'd taken from the private airstrip. A quick look inside confirmed what Nick had already suspected, that Joseito still had the keys. Pausing only long enough to grab a crowbar from the wall in his right hand—breaking open the ignition case would be faster than ripping out wires from behind the dash—Nick opened the car door quietly with his left hand and eased behind the wheel. He slammed the crowbar against the ignition until the silver cover splintered off. His heart pounding, Nick grasped the bare metal ignition and gave it a sharp turn. The motor should have started, but to his frustration it did nothing. Scowling, Nick tried again. Still nothing.

Swearing, he found the inside hood latch, popped the hood, and got out of the car. Intending to start the limo with the lead wire, he paused and glared down at the place where the distributor cap should have been. A string of swearwords left his lips.

"If that doesn't burn the ears off a nun, I don't know what will," said a low, sexy voice behind him.

Nick turned. Robyn was standing in the garage doorway, barefoot, her hair tousled, clad only in a sexy white satin gown that looked like something Greta Garbo would have worn. His glance raked over her, taking in the imprint of her nipples against the satin, and the way the material hugged her slender waist and thighs. His body pulsed to life. Had she not been holding a revolver, he would have said to hell with escaping.

Robyn's breasts shifted fluidly beneath the gown as she took in one deep bolstering breath after another. "You may as well give up," Robyn advised evenly. "There's no distributor cap. Joseito came back down and got it before we went to bed."

"Where is it?" Nick growled, furious to find himself thwarted after the daring escape he had made. And yet here he was, almost helpless, all the same, because there was no way a car would run without a distributor cap. Without the distributor cap, the spark plug wires had nothing to attach to. There was no way the piston could fire. Having a car without a distributor cap was like having a stagecoach without horses to pull it.

Robyn shrugged, the motion lifting and then lowering her breasts tantalizingly. "You'll have to ask Joseito that," she said calmly. "I have no idea where he put it. He figured you'd try something like this. Apparently, he was right," Robyn continued, closing the distance between them. Her arms were covered with goose bumps, and though the satin fabric of her gown was opaque, he could guess at the way she looked beneath it—round creamy breasts and rosy nipples, flat abdomen, and a triangle of dark, downy sable hair. He had the feeling she was pretty all over. So pretty, in fact, that Nick found himself wondering how many bullets she had in that gun.

"What about you, Robyn?" he asked softly as he walked backward, until he was propped against the garage wall. He crossed his ankles, his legs at a slant. "Are you telling me you didn't think I'd try something like this?" he asked, edging farther away in his attempt to distract her.

"Stop right there, Nick." The hand with the gun was shaking.

"Why?" he taunted softly, his gut instinct telling him she didn't have the callous disregard for human life that it took to shoot someone. He crossed his arms indolently at his waist as she took another step toward him. "What are you going to do if I don't?" he asked lazily, then lunged toward her, caught her wrist and gave it a sharp twist.

She cried out in pain. The gun fell to the cement floor. In one swift motion, Nick kicked it away from them, grabbed her by the shoulders and backed her up against the garage wall. All the anger and fear he'd felt over the past eight hours culminated in a blinding thirst for revenge. It was time Robyn got a taste of her own medicine, he thought. It was time she felt a little fear.

"I want that distributor cap," he growled.

Robyn angled her chin up defiantly. "Then you'll have to go to Joseito's room to get it. He put it under his pillow. He said it was the only way he could sleep."

Nick let his glance move over her tousled hair and soft, bare lips, before returning to her thick-lashed eyes. "But you didn't have any trouble sleeping, did you, Robyn?"

"I knew you were all right," she retorted defensively.

"All right?" Nick echoed, incensed. "You call being kidnapped at gunpoint all right? How would you like to be handcuffed?" He captured both her wrists and manacled them to the wall with his hands. "Doesn't feel so good, does it?" he rasped.

"Let me go." Robyn struggled furiously against him, her thighs nudging his.

"Like you let me go?" Nick asked, thrusting his weight against her.

"Nick, please," Robyn said. The softness of her breasts was crushed against the hardness of his chest. The apex of her thighs formed a vee to cup his swollen sex. Her pulse hammered in her throat, she sucked in several shallow breaths.

"Don't beg, Robyn," Nick said gruffly, irritated at the fear he saw in her eyes. Did she really think he would hurt her? "It doesn't become you."

Moisture gleamed in her eyes. Her tongue darted out to wet her lips. "Then what do you want from me?" she whispered.

"What I've wanted from the beginning." His gaze raked her again. Telling himself the little scare he intended to give her was nothing more than she deserved. "I want my freedom. Barring that—" Nick gave in to temptation and ran a hand down her jaw, tracing the beautiful line, then moved it to the soft, open seam of her bow-shaped lips "—a little something for my troubles." He kissed his way down her throat.

Trembling, she arched her neck and turned her head to the side. "Nick, no—"

"Too late," Nick murmured. Placing his hand beneath her chin, he brought her mouth swiftly, firmly back to his. His mouth came down on hers. He knew it was crazy. He could have had her gun, tied her up and been long gone by now, but all he wanted was one more taste of her sweet mouth. One more touch of her tongue. And even that wasn't enough.

She moaned her pleasure, and the struggling stopped. Nick had to touch her, see her. He started to draw down the strap of her gown.

"Hold it right there, Nick." Joseito's voice came out of nowhere. "Don't make another move."

Chapter Four

"Let her go, Nick," Joseito ordered harshly as Robyn nearly fainted with relief. Thank heaven her burly protector had come along when he did. Or who knew what might have happened, she wondered, drawing a shaky breath.

"And step away from Robyn slowly," Joseito said.

Reluctantly, with a deliberately sensual, almost taunting look in her direction, and another dark one in Joseito's, Nick did as ordered.

Joseito gave Robyn a carefully assessing look while her heart continued to beat double time. Nick was no longer touching her, but she could still feel his hands clamped over her wrists, his hard, hot mouth pressed to hers. He had touched her as if he knew exactly how she wanted to be touched. As if he knew instinctively how to arouse and please her.

"Are you all right?" Joseito asked Robyn gruffly, his craggy features contorted into a mask of concern.

Robyn nodded and released another long, tremulous breath. I can handle this, she thought. I can handle Nick. "Yes. I'm fine," she said with a smile.

But she knew even as she spoke that it wasn't really true. Nick's kiss had changed her, made her see that her life wasn't always going to be the same dull run-of-the-mill shade. His kiss had opened up her heart and soul and mind to the hopelessly romantic possibilities she had always dreamed and read and fantasized about, but never really felt existed.

The simple fact of the matter was, with his sexy smile, dark green eyes, his velvety voice and masterfully evocative touch, Nick Wyatt was a heartbreaker who had reputedly seduced many women. But, heaven help her, she was not going to be his latest victim. Especially when she had a job to do. If she didn't keep Nick out of Dallas, and he kept his promise to ruin Leland and interfered in company business, Leland's efforts to expand and strengthen the company would be lost. Leland would have no choice but to close down the Young Juniors line. Within weeks, everyone who worked on that line would be out of their jobs. And the new jobs that stood to be created by the expansion would also be lost.

Robyn had seen the toll it had taken on her own father when he'd become unemployed, and she wasn't about to let that happen to anyone else, not if she could stop it. Not when she knew she could reverse the situation almost single-handedly, simply by keeping Nick out of Leland's way a little longer, as Leland had asked.

Joseito spared a glance at the ignition on the limo. As his glance moved over the cracked and broken key slot, he swore in Spanish.

His disappointment over having their sensual interlude—and his imminent escape—interrupted, Nick inclined his head in Robyn's direction and sent her a sassy glance. "Now those are words you never hear in Spanish 101," he drawled lightly.

Robyn worked to suppress an answering grin. "I wouldn't know. I took French in school myself." But it figured Nick would know and understand all the major curse words. Probably in a variety of languages.

"Back upstairs, if you please," a grim-faced Joseito said as he glared at Nick with growing menace. Unlike Robyn, Joseito wasn't the least distracted by Nick's playfulness. "Now."

There was no denying either the lack of humor or the edge of impatience in Joseito's low voice. Again Robyn felt a prickle of unease, an awareness that, as Nick had already pointed out, she and Joseito both were doing something highly illegal. If Nick's own family hadn't requested it, she knew she never could have been talked into kidnapping him.

Nick frowned at Joseito, gave Robyn another narrow-eyed glance, then did as ordered.

Glad she had someone as big and strong as Joseito to enforce Nick's kidnapping, Robyn fell into step behind Joseito. As they marched toward the villa, she clenched and unclenched the hands at her sides, willing herself to relax. *Calm down. And think!* She was glad Joseito had come along when he did—and embarrassed, too, for what he had seen. Who knew what might have happened had Joseito not appeared when he did? Nick had seemed intent on making love to her, slowly and thoroughly, right there in the garage!

Whether or not he would have followed through was anyone's guess...or was that just wishful thinking on her part? She recalled how sensually and expertly he kissed...but the risk, the attraction, the chemistry between them, was still in there. And would continue to be, Robyn thought, as long as she and Nick were around each other, which wouldn't make her job easier. Or would it? Was it possible she might be able to control Nick with sex...or the hope of it? She wouldn't have to follow through on it, of course. She would never trade favors for personal gain. But Nick didn't know that about her. And whatever kept him in line would certainly help the overall situation.

Most of all, she wanted to avoid violence. She wanted Nick to want to be there, as much as Leland had assured her he eventually would.

In strained silence, the three moved up the stairs.

Robyn thought about the way the kidnapping had gone so far. She hadn't been much of a hostess, or Nick much of a guest. But that, too, could change. She could turn this whole sorry episode around...with just a little bit of clever handling and kindness.

Hands still raised to shoulder level, Nick sauntered reluctantly into his room.

As Robyn followed both Nick and Joseito into a bedchamber, she couldn't help but note with her expert clothier's eye that Nick's tuxedo looked very much the worse for the evening's exploits. There was a rip in one knee of the pants. Dirt smudged the jacket and shirt, and his tie had long been discarded. Unshaven, his hair a mess, he appeared both dashing and dangerous. Just looking at him, Robyn felt her heartbeat pick up the way it had in the garage, before, during and after his oh-so-sensual kiss. *Damn,* she thought, *I'm letting him get to me again.*

"Now what?" Nick said in a bored tone. Behind him, the sun inched higher in the sky.

Now what? Robyn struggled with the images that came promptly to mind of the two of them, cozily ensconced in his wide bed. That wouldn't do, even in fantasy, she told herself sternly.

Out loud, she advised him like a schoolmarm addressing a rowdy class, "I suggest you get some sleep, Nick."

He glanced at the bed. His lips compressed tightly. "I'll need sheets," he muttered with disdain.

Robyn thought about what he'd done to the last set of Porthault sheets and shook her head. "Sorry. No can do, Nick. But you did bring up a good point."

While Joseito continued to hold the gun on Nick, Robyn went into the adjoining bath and removed everything, including the towels. Returning, she tossed them out into the hall. Then she checked the closets, which were empty.

Joseito looked at Robyn. "This Nick is very resourceful, eh? Maybe it would be a good idea if we took his jacket and pants, too, just to be sure he not try and rappel down the side of the villa again.''

His eyes igniting with sudden temper, Nick flicked off his jacket and tossed it at Robyn. "The jacket you can have," he said with a fierce warning frown. "The pants, uncomfortable as they are, stay."

Joseito looked as he were about to protest. But Robyn knew even if Nick tore his pants and shirt into strips and made another rope, it wouldn't be enough to get him to the next floor, let alone the ground. "He can keep his pants on, Joseito," she said in a tone so calm it was almost bored. In fact it would be safer that way, she decided. Much safer. She didn't want to be around Nick if he was stripped down to his shorts. That was, if he even wore shorts.

Her mind was filled with images of his strong, muscled legs as she backed toward the door. Nick was staring at her just the way he had in the garage, right before he kissed her, with blazing sensual intent and unbridled energy.

Forcing her voice to remain even, to not think about what Nick might want to do with or to her at that moment, Robyn moistened her lips and said, "Sweet dreams, Nick."

He merely grunted in response and held her gaze. Boldly, deliberately. Robyn turned away quickly, her heart pounding.

She left the room without a backward glance. When she stepped into the hall, her hands were trembling. She clenched her fingers into fists.

Joseito backed out, locked Nick in, and pulled a chair up and set it outside Nick's door. "I think I will sit here for the time being," Joseito said as he settled his heavy weight on the seat. "Just in case Nick gets any more ideas."

Robyn breathed a sigh of relief. This unexpected "vacation" of Nick's had turned into a kidnapping and taken on a gritty realism more quickly than she had expected. Knowing, however, that thinking about what might have been wouldn't help, she pushed her regrets aside. "Good thinking, Joseito."

He studied her with the fond protectiveness of an older brother for a much younger sibling. "What are you going to do?" he asked gently.

Robyn shrugged. "First I'm going to call Leland and check in with him. Then I think I'll get dressed and go back into town, see what I can find there."

Joseito's dark brow furrowed. He looked at her as if she were taking an unnecessary risk. "We have food," he reminded her bluntly. "My brother, Carlos, is bringing it when he comes to fix breakfast."

"I know." Robyn smiled at Joseito companionably. "Leland told me we'd have a cook. I was thinking more in terms of clothes. Nick can't stay in that tux all week. I think he'd be far more comfortable in casual clothing."

Joseito's craggy features broke into a grin. He nodded at her with approval, letting her know that he didn't want Nick to be uncomfortable there any more than she did. "You have a big heart, Robyn," Joseito said softly.

Too big, Robyn sometimes thought. Because it was her heart, her wish not just to help but to protect hundreds of others, that had gotten her into this mess in the first place.

THOUGH IT WAS ONLY seven-thirty in the morning, Robyn got through to her boss on the first try. "Leland?"

"Robyn! I'm so glad you called. I've been waiting to hear from you."

Leland sounded as cheerful as Robyn was confused. Closing her eyes, she could imagine him sitting at his desk in the president's office of Wyatt & Company, his silver hair combed, his suit neatly pressed. Handsome and urbane, he had the kind of distinguished, almost fatherly manner that invited immediate confidences, as well as faith that those confidences would be kept.

"How are things so far?" he continued.

"Actually," Robyn answered with a sigh, wishing she had better news to impart, "the news is not as good as we'd both hoped it would be. Nick didn't want to come with us after all. In the end, Joseito and I had to kidnap him."

There was a brief, unhappy silence on the other end of the phone. "Is he hurt?" Leland snapped, sounding as fiercely protective of Nick as if he were his own son.

"No, but he's damned unhappy," Robyn reported.

There was another silence, a long one. "Well, considering how unhappy he's made his mother the past few days, first with the photos in that tabloid and then his threats to try to screw up a major business deal with a fight for control of Wyatt & Company, maybe that's the way it should be," Leland said gruffly.

On the one hand, Robyn knew how Leland—and indeed Cassandra Wyatt—must feel. The photo of Nick in bed with those four near-naked women had been shocking. His threats to oust Leland from not just Wyatt & Company, but also the Wyatts' Dallas home, were even worse. But still . . . would anyone really want to do this to their own child, no matter how unhappy they were with them? Distracting Nick and or talking him into laying off Cassandra's personal and business life was one thing. Kidnapping him for anything, even the most noble, selfless of reasons, was quite another.

"What about Cassandra?" Robyn asked as she felt herself begin to tense up even more. "Is she worried about Nick?"

"Why would she be?" Leland retorted casually. "She saw the two of you leave the symphony hall during intermission. She assumed . . . well, knowing Nick, you know what she assumed, Robyn, the same as I. That you would have no trouble leading him astray . . ."

And I didn't, not at first, Robyn thought as she recalled uncomfortably how easy it had been to catch Nick's eye. Was Leland right? Was she just another in a long line of women to catch Nick's male interest? Had he kissed all of them as passionately, thoroughly, and seductively as he had kissed her? Was she the only one to emerge from that kiss shaken and changed, or had others ... countless others ... felt the same way when confronted with Nick's incredibly sensual technique? "So Nick's mother knows what we did to Nick last night?" Robyn ascertained as she rubbed the tightness from the muscles in her neck.

"Of course she knows. She's the one who asked me to help arrange to get Nick out of town for a week or so, until our business is concluded and the scandal about his latest sexual exploit dies down, remember?"

"I know but ..." Robyn paused, remembering she had never actually talked to Cassandra Wyatt about any of this. Cassandra had personally sent her the symphony tickets. Cassandra had personally given her license to wear one of the couture dresses to the Meyerson Center. But Cassandra hadn't been the one who actually came out and asked her to shanghai Nick. Leland had, on his wife's behalf.

At the time it had seemed perfectly reasonable. Cassandra was woefully embarrassed about her only son's antics, and worried sick about his threats to embark on a public fight for control of the business his father had built. Even more distressing were the many jobs that would be put in unnecessary jeopardy if Nick succeeded with his plans. Cassandra wanted, as did Leland, Robyn, and all the others whose jobs might be at risk, time for Nick to calm down and think about the ramifications of his actions before he acted impulsively again. Leland was understanding, the perfect problem-solver and go-between. It was clear to all of them that Nick wouldn't take a vacation of his own volition, for the business's sake. So they'd tried to help him, on the QT. Unfortunately, they'd had to do it the hard way. The *potentially criminal* way.

"What is it, Robyn?" Leland asked gently. "I can tell something is bothering you."

Of course, something's bothering me! I'm not used to breaking the law, even for noble purposes, Robyn thought. She paused, clenched her hand tighter around the receiver, then confessed what had been nagging at her for hours now. Something that didn't make sense, considering the details of their plan. "Nick told me he had a meeting with his mother last night, after the symphony concert."

Leland made a sound like a smirk on the other end of the line. "Isn't that just like Nick," he ruminated skeptically.

Robyn frowned impatiently. "What does that mean?"

"Simply that there wasn't any meeting, not that I know of, anyway."

Robyn swallowed. "Are you sure?" She didn't know why exactly, but she so wanted to believe Nick was telling her the truth about this. About everything. "Is it possible that Cassandra could have set something up and not told you about it?" she probed.

"I don't see how," Leland said slowly, after another baffled silence, "since we were hosting a party at our home for the members of the Symphony League." He sighed harshly. "The truth of the matter is, given the circumstances, the negative publicity, the embarrassment of having her son exposed a playboy of limitless appetite, his all-too-public quarrel with me, and the way we're trying to not just save a troubled division of Wyatt & Company but expand it, Cassie really didn't want Nick at the house last night, period. In fact, she didn't want him at the symphony at all, for fear he might start in on the two of us there. That's why he was sitting with you, instead of with us. Had he not insisted on going, come hell or high water..." Leland's voice trailed off. Briefly, he sounded as unhappy about the drastic measures they'd had to take to get Nick out of Dallas as Robyn felt.

"Then why would he have told me he had to leave me because of a meeting with her?" Robyn persisted. Especially when everything, up to that point, had been going so well between them!

"Who knows what's on that Casanova's mind? Maybe he was setting up an easy out for himself. You know how he is with women, Robyn, kind of a hit-and-run guy."

And the last thing Robyn had ever wanted to be was a one-night stand for anyone.

"His exploits, as well as his appetites, are legendary, as that latest photo op attests," Leland continued conversationally.

"But if there was a meeting between Nick and his mother last night—" Robyn protested impulsively. *Something that would have patched up their difficulties and made this shanghaiing unnecessary.*

"If there was a meeting, if Nick were indeed in a reasonable frame of mind, then Cassandra would have asked me to call off the whole setup last night, Robyn. But she didn't. She asked me to get Nick out of town as quickly as possible, and I did so. If you would feel better talking to her personally, though, I will have her call you," he promised.

Cassandra Wyatt had always been somewhat unapproachable, even to the high-ranking staff of Wyatt & Company. First, because Nick's father ran the company, later because she was still grieving for her late husband. After their marriage, Leland had stepped in to actually run the company, making Cassandra's interaction with the staff unnecessary. Robyn was still a little uneasy around her, mostly because she didn't know her well enough to know how to approach her or talk to her as candidly as she talked to Leland. But maybe it was time that changed.

"Thanks, Leland." Robyn sighed her relief. "I think I do need to talk to her for my own peace of mind." If Nick's own mother told Robyn she wanted Nick here... then somehow it seemed all right. Kind of like baby-sitting a naughty child, Robyn thought, despite the technical illegalities of her actions.

"Of course you may speak with her about this if it will make you feel better," Leland soothed. "It'll be later tonight or tomorrow, of course—she's going to be wrapped up in financial meetings about the expansion all day and early this evening—but I will have her call you at the first opportunity."

"Thank you, Leland," Robyn said softly.

"It's I who should be thanking you, Robyn," Leland said kindly. "I can't tell you what a strain the last

few days have been, for both Nick's mother, and me."
Leland's voice caught. It was a moment before he
could go on. "With that disgusting tabloid still on
every newsstand in the city..."

Robyn knew what Leland meant about that. You
couldn't even buy a loaf of bread without seeing a naked Nick next to the checkout stand.

"Well, let's just say you're doing us both a big favor, keeping Nick out of Dallas this week. By the time
the two of you come back that tabloid will be off the
newsstand, the gossip about Nick and his exploits will
have quieted down, and Cassandra will be calm
enough to deal with Nick. Maybe then she can talk
him out of trying to wrest control of the company
away from us."

"You make it all sound so easy," Robyn said. As if
this hadn't turned into an incredibly complicated
mess.

"It is. Now, is there anything you need there that
you don't already have?"

"Some clothes for Nick."

"Of course. What an oversight on our part!"

"But I'm going to take care of that this morning,
first thing."

NICK STARED at the clothing Robyn held out to him,
but made no move to get up from his prone position
on the stripped bed. His arms folded behind his head,
he crossed his feet at the ankles and let his eyes rove
slowly over the multicolored shirt that was so bright it
made even a Mexican fiesta look dull, and baggy white

slacks that were big enough to house a whale. He didn't know what Robyn thought, but there was no way in hell he was wearing a shirt with big ugly parrots on it or those almost-bell-bottom pants. "You're kidding, right?" he drawled.

Briefly he saw a flash of hurt in her eyes and felt an involuntary pang of regret that was almost a reflex. For as long as he could recall, it had been drilled into him by his mother and his father that when someone was nice to you, you didn't throw their effort back in their face, no matter how inept or off target their actions. He still resented the hell out of Robyn for what she'd done to him, but he also felt for her in some strange way, too. Maybe because he had the feeling that none of this was her idea. It was more likely that she'd been suckered into helping Leland Kincaid, just as his mother had been suckered into switching her allegiance from family—and Nick—to Leland.

Nick didn't know what the man's charms were, how or even why Leland had accomplished what he had, but he knew this: he was staying until he did find out. There would be no more escape attempts, Nick had decided, only a concerted effort to sway Robyn over to his side, a concerted effort to get her to tell him everything she knew about Leland and whatever dirty tricks his new stepfather was up to. Then he could go to his mother, hopefully with Robyn and maybe even Joseito at his side, and talk some sense into her.

Her eyes still glimmering with hurt, Robyn adjusted the clothing in her palm, as if to get a better grip on the soft cotton garments. When she spoke again, however, her voice was as calm and soothing as a kindergarten teacher's. "I know the parrots are a little bright—"

"A little?"

"But I thought you'd like to be more comfortable, Nick."

Nick could only think of one definition of truly comfortable at the moment, and it involved Robyn, all five feet nine beautiful inches of her, himself and the wide bed he was lying on—sheets or no sheets. He wondered briefly what she'd do if he pulled her down beside him and kissed her senseless again. Would she melt in his arms as surely and sensually as she had the first time? he wondered, as blood rushed and pooled below his waist. Would she let him take things even further?

"I'm all for getting comfortable," Nick drawled with a slow smile. "But only if comfort means hauling me back across the border to the States," Nick finished.

Again, Robyn's expression was hurt, unsettled. She transferred the garments from her right hand to her left, then lifted her right hand to the silky sable brown hair curling over her shoulder. She brushed it back unthinkingly, her dark brown eyes trained on his face all the while. "Sorry, Nick." She sighed shortly, the abrupt movement briefly lifting her full breasts against the white cotton tank dress she wore. "You know we can't do that."

Nick let his eyes drift down the length of her slim short skirt to her bare knees and long, golden, sleekly curving legs. "I know you *won't,*" he corrected as he let his eyes move back up to the wide fire-engine red canvas belt she'd tied around her waist.

Robyn moved closer, her red espadrilles moving soundlessly over the ceramic tile floor. As she neared Nick, he could smell her perfume—a sexy, fresh, flowery scent. "Just try the shirt on," she persuaded.

As Nick gazed into her eyes, he realized that with precious little effort, Robyn might be able to convince him to do almost anything if he didn't keep his guard up. "Forget it," he advised shortly, reminding himself that it was Robyn's fault he was in this mess in the first place. "I'll stay in my tuxedo."

Robyn frowned and looked down her nose at him. "You really are a spoiled brat."

"Lady," Nick growled back, telling himself firmly he was not about to let her sweet-talk him into gleefully accepting this situation, no matter what she brought him, "you're about to find out how much of one." He scowled back at her, realizing that lack of sleep, combined with the tenseness of the situation, was about to make him lose his temper. Again. Only this time he wanted to do a lot more than shove her up against the wall and kiss her senseless to vent some of his pent-up frustration. This time, he wanted to make love to her, thoroughly and completely, until she was his captive, not the other way around.

But that wouldn't happen, either, Nick thought. Because he had more sense, and more class, than that.

Still seething at the situation, he bit out a warning. "Now get the hell out of here and let me get some sleep."

Robyn stared back at him, her eyes wide and innocently assessing, then left as quietly as she had come in.

Joseito—who'd seen and overheard the whole exchange from the portal—glared at Nick before following Robyn out the door.

Nick sighed. He knew he was behaving like an ungrateful jerk. He also knew his obnoxious behavior was the only shield he had against constant company. This was the one way he could buy himself time to think of a solution to his predicament.

If only there was a phone in his room, he thought. Some way he could notify his mother. She must really be livid with him now, Nick thought. There was nothing she hated more than missed appointments or unkept promises. And he had promised to meet her last night, party or no...

He must have fallen asleep, for the next thing he knew, Robyn was back, looking prettier than ever in the sexy tank-top dress, wide-brimmed straw hat, and espadrilles. The trusty Joseito was nowhere in sight. Nick wasn't particularly reassured about that. Knowing Joseito, he was just outside the bedroom door, waiting for the first hint of trouble, the first cry for help from the pretty Robyn....

"Okay, Nick, take a look at these." Robyn held out several plain white shirts. One buttoned up the front. One had a front placket and was designed to be slipped over his head. Both were made of untreated white cotton and matched the loose cotton trousers she had brought up earlier. Both looked infinitely more comfortable than the stiff, torn, dirty tuxedo pants and starched shirt he had on.

Nick tilted his head back to better see into her long-lashed eyes. Damn, if she didn't have the most beautiful face. Her soft bow-shaped lips were just right for kissing. He would like to kiss her again, if the situation between them was different, less complex.

Telling himself he had handled far worse situations than that in his years climbing mountains, flying jets and racing cars, Nick said softly, persuasively, "Both of us would be more comfortable, sweetheart, if you'd just switch allegiances and let me out of here."

"Forget it, Nick." She stepped back, her eyes alert to the growing danger.

"Why? I'd pay you, Robyn. I'd pay you very well. Hell, I'll even double what Leland's giving you."

Robyn thrust her lower lip out stubbornly. Her eyes turned flinty. "I already told you, it's not money I'm interested in, Nick. There's been no ransom asked for you, nor will there be."

Her self-righteous attitude only annoyed Nick further. "Then what do you want out of this?" he muttered, feeling the veins in his neck stand out. "What could you possibly get? Fame?"

Robyn knew it couldn't possibly be good for his face to turn that red. She attempted to comfort him hastily, "I want what your stepfather wants, Nick—what is good for the company."

Still struggling to hold on to his formidable temper, Nick shoved aside the garments she'd brought him and leapt to his feet. "Leland only wants what is good for himself," he said over his shoulder as he paced to the window and stood in front of it, sucking in long breaths of the invigorating salt air.

Robyn marched to his side and took up a post on the other side of the window frame. She kept her arms folded tightly in front of her and leaned a shoulder against the wall. "You don't know anything about him," she asserted quietly, her eyes on his. "Or me, for that matter."

No, Nick thought wearily, he didn't. "Then tell me," he urged softly. If he was ever going to find a way out of this situation, he had to know what was going on, and why. He was certain his kidnapping had something to do with Leland, and maybe the company, as well. What, precisely, Nick didn't know. As sly and crafty a devil as he was, Leland had to know that he couldn't keep Nick locked up indefinitely. Furthermore, once Nick's mother found out what Leland had done to her son, she would probably boot Leland out of not just the company, but the marriage, as well. Leland had to know that, Nick reasoned.

And yet, it seemed that Leland didn't really want Nick dead. If he did, he would have hired real henchmen, instead of just Robyn and Joseito.

A chill zoomed through Nick as the next possibility hit him with lightning speed. Was it possible that Leland wanted them all dead? That Leland was just cleverly setting them all up so he could one day blame Robyn and Joseito for the kidnapping plot? Or was there more going on than even Nick could guess thus far?

Robyn blew out an exasperated breath. "I'll tell you what you need to know when you need to know it. And not a moment before, Nick." She pushed away from the window and walked purposefully toward the bed. Snatching up the garments he'd carelessly discarded, she held them out to him expectantly. "Back to the shirts, Nick. Which one?"

Unable to care about what he wore—what Nick really wanted to know was how a woman as strong willed and moral as Robyn seemed to be had ever let herself get talked into kidnapping someone—he grabbed the slip-on shirt.

Robyn smiled and handed him the pants. Still looking more like an efficient schoolteacher than captor, she ordered, "Now try the clothes on."

Nick's mouth twisted with contempt. "Why?"

She widened her eyes at him sardonically. "So I can see if they fit."

Frustrated by the startling lack of choices in his life, Nick felt his insides clench. "Like it really matters if they do or not," he said.

Robyn tapped her foot and looked prepared to wait him out on this one indefinitely. "I'm not leaving until you try them on."

Despite his highly irascible behavior, a part of Nick didn't really want Robyn to leave, maybe because time seemed to pass so much more quickly when he was with her. He thrust the garments back at her. "Why not?"

"Because," she explained patiently, looking extremely satisfied with her purchases, "it's my job to see that you're both safe and comfortable this week, and I always do my job."

Nick found her allegiance to duty under the circumstances very ironic, to say the least. "Even if that job is a harebrained scheme that could have been cooked up in an 'I Love Lucy' rerun?" he queried with a smirk.

Looking oblivious to his patronizing manner, she merely pointed to the adjoining bath. "Go."

Nick thought briefly about stripping down in front of her, just to see the look in her eyes. Would she be shocked? Would she run like hell or sit there as still as a statue? Would she give him a lustful look or a condescending one?

Right now, Nick had to admit with a pained sigh of resignation, she looked as naive as a Girl Scout on a mission. Realizing that even he wasn't jaded enough to take advantage of such a moral innocent, he sent a look skyward. Why me? he asked silently.

Nick turned on his heel and stalked into the adjoining bath. He shut the door and peeled off his pants and shirt, then looked longingly at the glassed-in shower. Why the hell not? he thought, stepping out of his Jockey shorts. It might help him to feel better. It certainly couldn't make him feel any worse. And if Robyn didn't like it, who the hell cared?

He went inside the stall and turned on the tap. Seconds later, he was beneath the hot water and covered with fragrant soap.

Robyn pounded on the door. "Nick, what are you doing?"

He grinned and yelled. "Come in and see."

Silence fell as he fantasized pulling Robyn into the shower with him. Nick smiled, pleased with his ability to turn the tables on her even in this unfairly weighted situation. "Chicken?" he taunted.

The bathroom door slid open a fraction of an inch. Robyn said in a normal voice, "I'll wait out here for you, Nick. I still want to see those clothes."

"Then bring me a towel!" Nick demanded, irritated he hadn't provoked more of a rise out of her.

Seconds later, the door opened wider. Something blue and fluffy and soft flew in and landed on the floor outside the stall.

Pleased with the way he had taken back control of the situation, Nick showered another fifteen minutes, then shut off the water. To his dismay, instead of the towel he expected, there was a single blue washcloth on the bathroom floor. "What the—?"

Dripping wet, he picked up the washcloth, positioned it like a fig leaf over his privates and yanked the door to the bedroom open wide. Robyn was seated in a straight-backed chair, the hat over her lap. Her eyes widened with interest at the sight of him, enraged and dripping water, but she didn't move an inch from where she sat. Letting him know effectively, Nick thought, that the tables had turned again. More furious than ever with her, with the whole situation, Nick grated, "I said I wanted a towel!"

Robyn crossed her legs at the knees and smiled at him in a patronizing manner. "Under the circumstances, I felt a washcloth was less likely to be used as a lethal weapon, although judging by your expression, I can see I could be wrong about that. It may be we can't trust you with anything."

Nick glared at her. "You're right," Nick said calmly, drawing on every last bit of patience he had left. "I could rip this up into shreds and make a rope and try to tie your hands together behind your back, but I won't, if only because we both know that if I did that your trusty Joseito would not be far behind. I would still, however, like to dry off before I get dressed. So unless you want to handcuff me again and dry me off yourself, I suggest you get me a towel. A real one, this time."

Robyn studied him with an implacable look. "Make do with the washcloth, Nick. Either that, or air-dry." Without a backward glance, she sauntered toward the door and said in a faintly bored tone, "And call me when you're dressed again."

DECIDING HE WAS PAST the point of being a good sport about anything, Nick made no bones about complaining, "The clothes don't fit."

Robyn knelt before him, her hair spilling over her shoulders like raw silk as she tugged and measured the rough cotton covering his waist and thighs. "The pants are supposed to be loose, Nick."

He shrugged, wishing the sight of her kneeling in front of him wasn't so unbearably erotic. Especially since from his vantage point above her, he could see the rounded globes of her breasts swelling impudently out of the collar of her tank-top dress. Nick gritted his teeth. He was not going to give into his desire here. He was not even going to feel it.

"Call me crazy," he said bad temperedly. "I *like* my pants to stay up at the waist."

Before Nick knew what was happening, Robyn had bounded to her feet, vaulted across the room, yanked open the hall door and told Joseito, who was still stationed in a chair next to his door, "Joseito, some straight pins, please."

"Now what are you planning?" Nick asked dryly, letting none of the pleasure he felt just looking at Robyn enter into his voice. "Torture by acupuncture?"

"You only wish." Robyn grinned back at him with mocking disregard for his feelings.

Joseito came back with a small velvet cushion filled with straight pins. Robyn took a good look at Nick, the temper and the desire simmering deep inside him, then inclined her head toward the straight-backed chair. "Joseito, why don't you sit in here for a change? I think Nick and I could both use the company."

Meaning, she doesn't trust me an inch, Nick thought as Joseito complied.

"Okay, Nick, lift the hem of your shirt," Robyn ordered.

What did she think he was? Some damned Ken doll for her to play with? She fastened on the recalcitrance in his gaze and said quietly, "Do you want the waist of your pants fixed or not?"

There'd be nothing helpful about having his trousers pool around his ankles, Nick thought.

"Fine. Fix it." Making no effort to hide his annoyance at the bothersome task—why couldn't she have simply bought pants that fit without needing alternation?—Nick sighed loudly and lifted his shirt. The next thing he knew, her hands were on him, measuring and molding the fabric to his waist.

Robyn tightened the waistband and slipped her hand inside the cloth, between the pants and his skin. Nick fought a shiver as a wave of heat washed through him in undulating waves. Much more of this, he thought as the lower half of him came to life with disturbing quickness, and there would be no doubt in her mind about his real feelings for her.

Fortunately for them both, Robyn worked quickly. Professionally.

Once the fabric was secure, she stuck a pin into the fold, then moved around to the other side. "How does this feel?" she asked, after she had similarly tucked the other side.

Nick didn't know about the pants. He couldn't concentrate a whit on the pants. Her hands, however, were the warmest, softest, silkiest hands he'd ever felt caressing his bare skin. He stared at the opposite wall and refused to meet her eyes. "Feels okay," he said.

The next thing he knew, Robyn was on her knees in front of him again. At eye level with the burgeoning tension in his crotch, she slid one hand into the front of his waistband, and the other down the inside of his left thigh. Frowning, she smoothed her hand across the fabric and murmured distractedly, "I don't like this inseam. It's a good one or two inches too low, but it can be fixed."

Removing another pin from the cushion, she used it to mark the planned adjustment on his inseam.

Finished, she got lithely to her feet. Nick didn't know if she had noticed the changes in his anatomy, which had started and grown markedly with the intimacy of her touch, but he was achingly aware of his throbbing lower half. In fact, he figured he'd be aching for the next several hours to come.

Damn, she could turn him on, and without even half-trying. It must be the lack of sleep, he told himself, the strain, and no decent food. Once he had eaten and slept, he'd be able to curtail these crazy thoughts about his beautiful female captor. Because that's all she was to him. The crazily mixed-up woman who had gotten him into this mess.

BY THE TIME Robyn got back to her own room, where she'd set up a portable sewing machine to do the alterations on the clothes she'd bought for Nick, her hands were shaking and her bones were weak. Those photos of Nick in *Naughty Not Nice* had not lied. Nick had a beautiful body and, considering the way his body had just reacted to her slightest touch, a very strong sexual drive.

He also cleaned up amazingly well, except for the day's growth of beard. As she began to sew, she made a mental note to try to get him an electric razor so he could shave, and a toothbrush and toothpaste, too. He would probably also need underwear, shoes, maybe even a swimsuit as the week dragged on and he became more accustomed to the idea of his unexpected stay at the villa. She had a lot yet to do to make him comfortable. Despite the circumstances, she wanted this to be a vacation for Nick. A pleasurable holiday...

Robyn frowned as she finished one seam and started on another. If only Nick wasn't such a ladies' man, and so darned untrustworthy, if only she hadn't been talked into luring him away for a week and then been forced to follow their worst-case scenario, she might actually consider getting involved with him. But she had done all that, and Nick was furious with her, as anyone in his position would have every right to be. So an involvement was out. She had to keep her distance. Had to.

Chapter Five

"Leland, you will never believe this," Cassandra Wyatt Kincaid moaned on a beleaguered sigh as she stormed into his den. "Never in a million years!"

"Believe what, dear?" Leland asked casually, looking up from the stack of Wyatt & Company financial reports he was reading.

"The message Nick left for me late this morning, with one of the maids. It says, 'Sorry about missing our appointment last night, Mom. Something came up.'"

Leland studied Cassandra carefully. His wife looked very upset. That wasn't unexpected. Nick had been giving her fits, even before he had disappeared. "And that's all it says?" Leland questioned calmly, although he already knew full well what the message was, since he had been the one to leave it for her.

"Yes. Apparently, that was it." Cassandra twisted the message in her hands, folding and unfolding it. "He hung up before the maid could get a phone number where he was staying."

Leland took a small sip of iced tea and put the glass soundlessly down onto the table beside his chair. He had been right to curtail his day at the office and come home directly after lunch. Cassandra needed him. And he needed to be here, to prevent anything unexpected from cropping up and spoiling his plans. "That's too bad," Leland said. He reached over to pat his wife's hand sympathetically. "It would've been nice to know if he was still in the city."

Cassandra frowned and smoothed the row of buttons down the front of her periwinkle blue suit. "He is," she said firmly, then amended, "at least he was this morning."

Why the hell did she think that? Leland felt sweat gather beneath his collar. He picked up the pen he'd been using and fingered it idly. Barely sixteen hours into the plan, and already things were going awry. "What do you mean?" he asked.

Cassandra withdrew her hand from his, took two steps to the right and sank down into the wing chair opposite him. "The call was local."

Leland paused to look into the fire roaring in the grate. "How do you know that?"

Cassandra grinned at him triumphantly. "I phoned Harvey McMillan over at the phone company."

Leland struggled to keep his expression calm. "Is Harvey permitted to tell you something like that?" he asked, wrinkling his brow.

"Officially, no. But I called in a few favors—I helped him and his wife out when they ran into trouble planning a benefit for Children's Hospice a few years ago—and got him to run an unofficial check on the incoming calls this morning. As it turned out, there were only two. One from the dry cleaners, and that was accounted for, and one from a phone booth downtown.''

Leland placed his elbows on the arms of the wing chair and clasped his palms together. He wished he was drinking brandy now, instead of the iced tea the Dallasites seemed to drink winter or summer. He smiled at his wife benevolently. ''So you think Nick's still in the city?'' he asked carefully, trying to make it sound as if he cared deeply.

Fortunately, she was too caught up in her own feelings to realize the manufactured nature of his.

''It certainly appears that way, doesn't it?'' Cassandra remarked bitterly as she stood and dashed an angry tear from her cheek.

Leland watched his wife restlessly pace the luxuriantly appointed room once again. ''I wonder why Nick didn't arrange another meeting with you this morning then,'' Leland remarked gently.

''That's just it!'' Cassandra retorted with so much maternal agitation that for a moment Leland felt his heart go out to her. ''Nick should have called me today! He should have come to see me! He knew how important it was we discuss the future of the company.''

''You're absolutely right. Nick should have been here,'' Leland agreed wholeheartedly. ''If not last night, then this morning.'' He sighed his regret, then commiserated gently, "But you know how Nick is, Cassie dear. He sees a pretty girl, and wham!"

Cassandra played with the single strand of pearls around her neck. "He was sitting with Robyn Rafferty last night!"

"Isn't she one of our employees?"

"Yes, you know her. She's the one I had planned to promote, right before I stepped down as president and gave the reins of the company over to you. You talked me out of it, because you felt she needed another six months or so on the regular lines, working for our other top designers, before we gave her her own imprint in the Junior department."

"Oh, yes," Leland murmured, pretending to suddenly recognize who Robyn was, though he had paid attention to Robyn the moment he first stepped foot in Wyatt & Company as an outside consultant, for it was clear she was the hope for the future of the company, as well as the star of all the junior and senior designers they employed. He knit his brows together. "Have you talked to Robyn today?" She better not have, he thought.

"I called her at the office." Cassandra shrugged and briefly looked all the more distressed. "Apparently, she's on vacation. No one knows how or where she can be reached, just that she's not due back until next week at the earliest."

Thank God, he'd had enough time to set this up well, Leland thought. He worked to disguise his relief at having managed to keep the two women from comparing notes on the situation. "Have you tried Ms. Rafferty at home?"

Cassandra shook her head. "No answer. I left a message on her machine to call me, but... unless she checks in..."

"Which might be unlikely if she's on vacation," Leland murmured.

"Exactly." Cassandra sighed her resignation.

Leland shrugged. "Perhaps that's just as well, though," he remarked cautiously. Cassandra sent him a sharp look. He continued, using the gentle husbandly tone he had perfected over the past twenty-five years. "Darling, it might be awkward, asking an employee about Nick. What would you say? *Have you seen my son? Did you bed him?*"

"Leland!" Cassandra's fair cheeks turned bright pink.

Leland put his papers aside, stood and gathered Cassandra in his arms. "Sorry, darling, but you know how Nick's mind works. Everyone does. Robyn Rafferty is a very beautiful young woman. Everyone saw Nick and Robyn together at intermission. After which, neither of them came back in."

Cassandra swallowed and rested her head on his shoulder. She smelled of the extravagantly rich perfume she favored. "You really think Nick seduced her, don't you, Leland?" she said in a hushed tone.

Leland shrugged and didn't answer. Better to let some things go unsaid.

"Damn Nick anyway!" Cassandra said. Balling her hand into a fist, she punched Leland's shoulder in impotent rage. "Isn't it enough that he didn't show up last night when he had promised me he would? Did he have to put the moves on one of our most valued young employees, too?"

"Now, Cassie," Leland cautioned, using the familiar nickname he had given her. "We don't know that for sure."

Cassandra spun away from him in a rage. "Don't we?"

Leland followed his wife through the room. She was such a beautiful woman, he thought, it was almost a shame he couldn't love her. Really, he couldn't love anyone. Only what they could give him. And in the end, it always seemed even that wasn't enough, for he always had to have more. "Robyn is a levelheaded young woman," he said.

Cassandra whirled around, looking more upset than ever. "She's not *used* to men like Nick."

True, Leland thought, that was what had made it all so perfect. Robyn wouldn't know quite how to handle Nick, but at the same time, was innocent enough to be afraid of him, to not trust him an inch, no matter how much he pleaded or cajoled. Nick, on the other hand, with his jaded past but oh-so-chivalrous soul, was likely to be very drawn to Robyn. "Nick will get his life straightened out," Leland reassured his wife.

"When?" Cassandra asked miserably as she briefly lifted both hands to shield her face. "Oh, I know he was hurt when his father died. I know he was angry with me when I married you. But honestly, Leland, did he have to retaliate by threatening to take away con-

trol of the company? After he had already rejected my
offer to run the company in his father's stead?''

''Maybe he's already had second thoughts about
trying to oust me from my job.''

Cassandra slowly dropped both hands to her sides.
She studied Leland, her face becoming guardedly
hopeful once again. ''You think that's why he didn't
show up?''

''It could be,'' Leland said, knowing that by the end
of the week this was all going to be a moot point anyway. When he was through with his business deal-
ings, there'd be nothing left for mother and son to
fight over. He shrugged and continued, making up his
theories as he went along—anything to please Cassie
and calm her down at this point. ''Maybe he's
ashamed of the way he's behaved lately. Maybe he realized it would be better for all of us if he just lay low
for a while, at least until the tabloid is off the stands.''

Cassandra took a moment to digest that. She absently patted her well-coiffed hair into place. ''I wish
I could talk to Robyn,'' she said slowly at last, as she
began to pace the room once again. ''I wish I could
find out what Nick's frame of mind was last night. We
had so little time together before the concert. . . .''

Very little, Leland thought. He had seen to that.
And good thing, too. If Nick and his mother had had
more than the brief five minutes together, they might
have begun to work through the strain that had
haunted their relationship since Cassandra's marriage
to Leland. And that would have ruined everything,

Leland thought. Because then Nick and Cassandra might have begun to really talk, compare notes.

Realizing abruptly that his wife was waiting for some sage advice from him, Leland soothed, "I'm sure it'll all work out, given time. You and Nick will patch things up." *But not until after I'm long gone...*

"I hope so."

"I know so, darling." Leland took Cassandra into his arms and held her close. A few more days. That was all he needed, and then everything he wanted would be his.

"WELL? WHAT DO YOU THINK?" Robyn asked.

The truth was, the trousers Robyn had purchased for him at the open-air market seemed as if they had been tailor-made for him, now that she'd worked on them herself. But he'd be damned if he'd tell her that, Nick thought, since she was responsible for his being here in the first place. After fewer than twenty-four hours, he was already climbing the walls. He couldn't imagine staying here indefinitely, or even so much as another day. He wasn't used to being cooped up. Wasn't used to having someone else call the shots for him.

He'd spent the past couple of hours—while she was messing around, sewing his pants—thinking of how he could turn the situation around to his favor. The best way, of course, would be to convince Robyn that she'd done wrong, that she needed to tell him why and how this had all come about—he was willing to bet it hadn't been her idea—and then let him go. How to accomplish that, though, he didn't know. Every time he looked at her and thought about what she and Joseito had done to him, his temper flared and nearly got the best of him. And that, too, was unusual. Usually, women didn't make him wish he could simultaneously wring their necks and kiss them senseless. But that's what he felt for Robyn. Sizzling desire. And resentment.

Aware she was still waiting for an answer, he turned his attention back to the pants he'd slipped on, studied them briefly, then allowed, "They're okay."

Robyn breathed a soft, sexy sigh of relief. Her strong desire to please him confused Nick, too. Why should she care if he was happy or comfortable or not? The woman had kidnapped him!

Robyn stepped closer. "You're sure?" She peered at him closely, studying his face. "The waist isn't too tight or too loose now, is it?"

"I told you, it's fine," Nick repeated impatiently, pushing the words through his teeth as he struggled to contain his soaring emotions.

Robyn blinked, looking stunned and hurt by his gruffly condescending tone. Once again, Nick felt a flash of guilt. He had not been raised to treat people this way, even his adversaries. *You master your enemies not by force, but by forgiveness,* his mother had always said. Well, maybe now was time to put that wise old saying to the ultimate test, Nick thought. If he could forgive Robyn, if he could get rid of some of this anger, then maybe he could get on with the business of finding a way out of here.

Nick willed himself to forget the kidnapping, to pretend it had never happened, that he was here with Robyn of his own free will, and simply start over with her again. I can do this, he said to himself. I *have* to do this.

Swallowing hard, Nick attempted a polite tone. "Thanks," he said, surprised to hear how even his voice could sound when he was under so much stress, "for going to all the trouble. I uh . . ." *Be nice now, remember?* "I appreciate it."

Robyn jerked her head back, as if by looking at him at another angle, she would be better able to understand him. Finally, seeing how hard he was trying to be civil, she said, "You're welcome, Nick." She idly fingered the yellow measuring tape she had looped around her neck. "I just want you to know I'm sorry this worked out the way it did."

Then let me go—*now,* Nick thought. But realizing it was futile to try to persuade her via argument to help him and not Leland, at least at this point, Nick merely shrugged and said calmly, "We all have to do what we have to do." He paused and looked directly into her eyes. "I understand that, Robyn."

Do you? her eyes said.

As he held her gaze, Nick wished fervently they had met some other time, some other way. If they had, it would have been so easy for him to pursue her.

He nodded at his newly tailored pants. "Where did you learn to sew like this?"

Robyn smiled fondly, as if that question kindled only happy thoughts. "My mother bought me a kiddie sewing machine and taught me how to follow a pattern and make clothes for my dolls when I was in the third grade. By the time I was in junior high, I was making some of my own clothes. By the time I was in high school, I never wore anything I didn't design and sew."

Nick whistled softly, impressed. "You must've saved your parents a bundle on clothes," he teased, liking the way her sable eyes lit up when she talked about her work.

Robyn grinned. She tugged at the yellow tape measure around her neck, until it came loose. Holding the end in one hand, she used the other to curl the tape into a tidy little ball.

"Actually, it was quite the opposite."

Entranced, both by the efficient rhythm of her soft-looking hands and the low, sexy timbre of her voice, Nick waited for Robyn to go on.

"Since sewing and designing was all I wanted to do, I was always in need of material and thread and bias tape." Robyn secured the end of the tape, then held it in her palm. "They got used to it, though."

"I take it you studied design in college?"

Robyn nodded. "At the Parsons School of Design in New York."

So he was right. She wasn't a common criminal, but someone who had been sucked into this calamity every bit as unexpectedly as he had, Nick thought. Wanting to know more about her, what drove her, Nick pressed, "And yet you came back to Texas to work."

Robyn lifted a slender shoulder. "Texas is my home."

Nick's gaze fastened on the golden sheen of her bare arm. Realizing he was letting his thoughts wander again, he jerked his gaze back to hers and once again gave their conversation his full attention. "Ever wish you'd done something else?"

Robyn bit into her lower lip thoughtfully. "To tell you the truth," she said softly, settling into a nearby straight-backed chair and crossing her legs demurely at the knee, "I can't imagine ever having done anything else." Her eyes still on his face, she tugged her skirt a little lower. "What about you? Do you regret your foray into race-car driving?"

Nick pulled up a chair opposite Robyn and sank into it backward. "At the moment, yes." He folded his arms across the back of the chair. "Somehow I think if I'd been in Dallas all along, my stepfather never would have been named president of Wyatt & Company."

"You may be right about that." Robyn frowned, looking uncomfortable again. "Then again, you might not be. Your mother said you've never had any interest in the family business."

"It's true. Up until now, I haven't. But all that's changed," he said fervently, wondering how he would ever convince her it was true, when his actions in the past had been so contrary.

Robyn's delectable lower lip twisted wryly. "Somehow I can't imagine you living and dying by what is reported in *Women's Wear Daily*," she said.

Damn, but she intuited a lot about him, Nick thought. "I suppose you read it religiously," Nick guessed.

"Every issue," she confirmed with a smile that soon turned sad.

"What's the matter?" Nick asked.

"Nothing. I'm just a little homesick for the States, I guess. I miss the little things, like reading *USA Today* and my own special brand of amaretto coffee."

"Didn't bring any with you?" he asked sympathetically.

"Nope. Just clothes, toiletries, and a hair dryer."

"That's reason enough for me to go back to Dallas," Nick said.

Robyn tossed him a wry look. "I can live without my amaretto coffee, Nick, and if I have to, even *WWD* and *USA Today*." Her eyes, serious and apologetic now, met his. "What I can't and won't pass up is my chance to help your mother and stepfather secure the future of Wyatt & Company."

Nick stared at her, confused. "What are you talking about?"

"The firm's in financial trouble, Nick."

"It can't be! My father only died a year ago. Wyatt & Company was rock solid then."

"A lot's happened in a year. The economy took another nosedive. Sales are sluggish at best. Plus, the firm had no clear-cut leadership until Leland came along."

"My mother was at the helm."

"At least in the beginning, she was grief stricken and unable to cope. She delayed on making a lot of decisions, Nick, decisions that should have been made promptly. After a few months, she recovered and began working up to speed again, but the initial damage was done. While our competitors had already come up with new, different and exciting things to tempt consumers into spending again, Wyatt & Company had only cranked out the same old things. It was a bad six months or so, Nick. A very bad six months."

"You're saying we're in danger of losing the family firm?"

"To keep it solvent, you either have to forge ahead or cut back. Your mother has decided to move forward, and she's doing that by handing the reins of the company over to Leland."

The depth of Robyn's naiveté where his charming stepfather was concerned grated on Nick's nerves. "And you think Leland is just the man to take my father's place as CEO?" he asked Robyn bitterly.

Robyn shrugged. "Someone has to take charge. Your mother thinks it should be Leland. I trust her judgment, Nick."

Nick shook his head in disgust. "You don't know anything about the man, not really, and neither does my mother."

Robyn quirked a brow. "I know I don't want to hear your version of things," she said mildly.

"He threatened me, Robyn."

"Leland wouldn't do that," she said firmly.

Nick's hands tightened on the top of the chair. "What makes you so sure of that?"

"Because I know him!" Robyn said as she bolted out of her chair and began to pace the room agitatedly. "I've worked closely with him! I've never seen him be anything but kind to anyone."

Nick stood and followed her to the window. "You call masterminding my kidnapping kind?"

Robyn whirled to face him, the sharp movement leaving him awash in the scent of her perfume. "We all hoped you'd come willingly," Robyn countered, crossing her arms at her waist. "And he was only doing it to spare your mother further embarrassment. She was horrified by the tabloid photos."

"As Leland wanted her to be. Can't you see how he's manipulating you? How he's manipulating everyone?" Nick asked.

Robyn stared out at the azure blue gulf. "What I see is you blaming everyone but yourself for your current misfortune," she countered stonily.

It was clear she'd been brainwashed against him. His disappointment in Robyn's lack of faith in him cut much deeper than he expected.

He had to steer away from the emotional and concentrate on the facts. Maybe if he could get her to focus on the facts concerning Wyatt & Company business, she'd begin to see there were enough holes in Leland's story to sink a ship.

"Have you ever asked yourself why Leland is now in charge of the company, through the power of attorney my mother gave him?" Nick asked casually.

"My mother could easily have continued on as CEO. I know she had a hard time in the beginning, but she had recovered and she was doing fine before Leland appeared on the scene."

"Whether she could have continued to handle the job of running the company alone or not is a moot point, Nick. Your mother wanted her new husband involved in the family company at an executive level, and Leland graciously accommodated her."

"You mean, he robbed her of control of her company," Nick said.

As before, whenever he tried to talk some sense into her, Robyn ignored him. "What we need to focus on is the future, Nick."

Nick felt his lips twist into a bitter smile. "What future?"

"Your future as a race-car driver."

"Or in other words," he guessed, "I should stay out of Wyatt & Company business."

Robyn dropped her arms and drew a deep breath. She looked him straight in the eye. "I think that would be best for all concerned, yes."

Silence fell between them. Once again, Nick realized Robyn meant him no harm, she was only doing as she had been schooled to do. But by whom? Had it just been Leland? Or had it taken, as he was beginning now to suspect, someone even more compelling to talk Robyn into becoming involved in something so shady? Someone close to him?

On impulse, Nick asked, "Who talked you into doing this, Robyn?" She said nothing, merely assumed a mulish look, and he continued, "Was it just Leland? Or was it my mother, too?"

She didn't have to answer; he saw the acknowledgment in her eyes, the moment he spoke his mother's name. Nick swore profusely and stalked away.

Robyn remained at the window, watching him uneasily. "I'm sorry, Nick."

"So my mother is in on this!" he said unhappily. Not waiting for Robyn to answer him, he continued, "Not that it should be any surprise to me, I guess. She was furious enough with me the last time..."

"What last time?" Robyn blurted out. She touched a hand to her lips. "You mean you were in bed with four women before?"

"No," Nick turned and strode toward her aggressively, the timbre of his steps matching his mood. "But I was on the front page of a tabloid. It was a long time ago, when I was dating Suzy Merrick—"

"The model."

"Right. I went to pick her up for a date one night and just as we were walking out of her New York apartment, we saw this guy spray shaving cream all over my car. I grabbed him by the front of his shirt and hauled him off the car. He let loose of the shaving cream can, and then bingo, this reporter stepped out from a delivery truck and snapped a photo of me grabbing the guy while my date looked on, her expression suitably horrified. It turned out the whole thing had been a trap, of course. The photo hit the front page of a tabloid. The guy I grabbed tried to sue me for assault. My lawyers threatened to countersue, and the whole thing died down, but not before my mother and father were horribly embarrassed. Since then, I have tried to keep a low profile. Or as low a one as I could keep, given my profession. But at least I managed to stay out of the tabloids.''

"Until earlier this week.''

"Yeah.'' Nick was silent, gloomy.

"Did you and your mother argue about the picture last week?'' Robyn asked.

Nick glanced up, surprised Robyn would have to ask such a thing. But then, his mother was a private person. She wouldn't have discussed family matters with an outsider.

"That's putting it lightly. She was still so furious she could hardly speak when I saw her before the symphony last night. We only had about five minutes to talk.'' Nick sighed his regret, remembering. "I wanted to talk about it then, but she didn't want to start what was very likely going to be an emotional discussion right before we went out for the evening, so she said we'd talk about it later, after the symphony. Only, as you know now, I never got the chance.''

He'd never had the opportunity to show her the copy of the hospital emergency room records that backed up his story. If he could show his mother those hospital records, she'd at least listen to him about the tabloid photos, and if she listened to him about that, then she might begin to pay attention to him when he told her everything that Leland had done to him, starting with the threats, the set-up tabloid photo, and now the kidnapping, as well. Surely, Nick thought, if his mother knew everything that had been going on, she would stop being angry at him and begin to see her new husband for the sleazy operator he really was.

"Please, Robyn. I could clear this whole mess up if I could just talk to my mother," Nick said. He was pleased to note for the first time Robyn actually looked amenable to one of his suggestions. Was it possible that she was at least beginning to doubt some of the things Leland had told her?

"She's supposed to call either later this evening or first thing tomorrow," Robyn said.

"Why wait?" Nick pressed home his advantage before Robyn could think better of her decision. "Why not now?"

Robyn shook her head. "She's in important business meetings all day."

"Wait a minute. I thought Leland was running things now," Nick said.

"He is. With your mother's assistance. She may have stepped down and handed over most of the responsibility for day-to-day operations to Leland, but she's still involved in a supervisory capacity."

"To the point where she knows everything that's going on?" Nick asked.

"Everything important," Robyn confirmed. "Which is why I don't think we should interrupt her, when we know she's in meetings that are crucial to the betterment of the company."

Nick sighed. He didn't want to make things any harder for his mother than they already were. She had been embarrassed enough, though through no fault of his own. They were talking about waiting another few hours, that was all. "You will let me talk to her when she calls?" he asked tensely.

Robyn nodded. "I promise. If you want to get some sleep in the meantime—"

"Impossible," Nick growled as he resumed his pacing. He felt like a caged animal!

"You're restless?"

He rounded on her, wishing she didn't look so pretty with the late afternoon sunlight streaming in, illuminating her hair. "Wouldn't you be in my place?"

Robyn smiled at him mysteriously, looking once more like a Girl Scout on a mission. "Then perhaps it's time we did something about that."

"ISN'T THIS GREAT?" Robyn asked half an hour later.

Nick shook his head. "Watching Katharine Hepburn in *On Golden Pond* is not exactly my idea of boredom-ending entertainment," he said. Then, realizing he was clenching his teeth, he forced himself to relax his shoulders and neck. Why hadn't his mother called? How much more of this enforced isolation and captivity could he take?

Robyn gestured good-naturedly at the movies stored in the cabinets along one wall before taking a bag of popcorn out of the microwave. She tore open the top and poured the steaming buttered popcorn into two large bowls. "If there's something you'd rather see, just let me know and we'll put it in after we watch this."

Nick grimaced as Robyn went about fixing them each an icy cola. It seemed all he'd done the past twenty-four hours was sit. How the hell was he supposed to concentrate on a movie when he was going crazy waiting for his mother to call? He looked at the row of movie videotapes lined up along one wall. "You really want to watch two movies back-to-back?" he asked incredulously, not bothering to hide his impatience with waiting.

Robyn smiled at him brightly. She handed him a bowl and a drink, then went back to get hers. "Why not? After all, how often do you have a chance to watch movies in your own little theater?"

"Anytime I want," Nick muttered, as a new surge of uneasiness twisted in his gut. What if his mother didn't call? What if she didn't believe him, or even want to listen to him, when she did? God knows, if she was angry enough to have had him shanghaied and taken out of the country, she wouldn't be too keen on anything he had to say. He would have to make his mother listen to him. He would clear this all up, expose Leland for the conniving bastard that he was.

At Robyn's curious look, Nick elaborated reluctantly, "We've got a state-of-the-art video room at my mother's home in Dallas."

Robyn blinked, amazed. She watched as Nick shoved his fingers through his hair. "Really? With a big screen and tiered seats? Right in your house?"

"Right in our house," Nick confirmed as Robyn brought her own bowl of popcorn and glass of cola back to her seat. She sat down beside him in a cloud of sexy perfume.

"So... you never went to the movies with your friends?" Robyn asked as she dug into the popcorn with gusto.

"Of course I did," Nick said humorlessly. He hadn't been that cossetted!

Robyn picked up the remote control, paused the film and rewound it to the point where she'd gotten up to make the popcorn. Letting the film stay on that frame momentarily, she turned to him and asked, "Why did you go out to see a movie if you already had a theater in your house?"

"Because the object was to get *out* of the house, as much as to see the movie. And we didn't see first-run films at home, only ones that had been around a while."

"I see." Robyn grinned at him flirtatiously before taking a long draft of cola. "You're a restless type, aren't you?" she teased.

"Very," Nick said, meaning it. The more he was around her, the more restless he got.

Robyn held his gaze a moment longer, then went back to watching the movie. Nick tried to focus on it, but as the fatigue of the past twenty-four hours caught up with him, he kept nodding off. The next thing he knew, the movie was over and Robyn was dabbing tears from her eyes. "Wasn't that the most wonderful movie you've ever seen?" she asked in a husky voice still choked with emotion.

"I don't know." Nick yawned and stretched. "I've never seen it."

"You haven't!" Robyn said, amazed.

Nick shrugged. Despite her reaction to the film, he still wasn't convinced he had missed anything.

Robyn gathered up their empty bowls and glasses. "Well, we'll have to watch it again, when you're awake this time."

Spare me the melodrama, Nick thought. If there was anything he couldn't stand it was movies that made people cry. "Your turn to pick," Robyn said.

"We're really going to watch two movies back-to-back."

"Got any better way to pass the time while we wait for your mother to phone?"

Yes, Nick thought, though none of them were workable, as they all involved a bed, Robyn and him. "We could call my mother."

"I think it would be better to wait, Nick." Robyn scanned the movie titles for the next selection. She turned to him, looking extremely satisfied both with his newfound cooperation and her latest toy. "Besides, for you it will only be like watching one movie since you slept through the first one."

Nick got lazily to his feet. He knew he should be furious with Robyn for keeping him cooped up this way, but the more time he spent with her, the less aggrieved and resentful he felt. "How about a comedy?" Nick scanned the titles on the shelves, finally focusing on one that appealed to him. "They've got Steve Martin's *Roxanne.*"

"Oh, I love that movie!" Robyn said.

Nick grinned. He had loved it, too. "Martin should have had an Oscar for that one," he said as he pulled it out of the stack. Was it the nap that had relaxed him and started to untie the knot in his gut, or simply the process of being with her?

The film had not been rewound. Nick slid it into the VCR and punched reverse.

"I agree. He must really be a very romantic man at heart," Robyn continued in a voice that was soft with approval.

Nick quirked a brow. This movie business was quickly becoming profitable, if only because it relaxed her enough to allow him to gather more information. "You're romantic, too, I gather?" Nick asked softly. *I should have guessed.*

Robyn smiled at him unabashedly. "Very."

"So why aren't you married?" Nick asked as Robyn checked the film and saw it was still rewinding.

Robyn struggled to contain her nervousness. "What makes you think I'm not?"

Nick inclined his head in the direction of her lap. "No ring on your left hand."

She turned to him, the hint of a pleased smile on her face. "You are observant."

Lady, Nick thought, tearing his peripheral gaze away from the swelling softness of her breasts beneath the tank-top dress, you don't know the half of what I've noticed about you. Not that he should be thinking of the sexiness of her long, slim legs, trim ankles and tiny waist.

Telling himself it was just his curiosity he was trying to satisfy now, Nick asked, "Ever been married?"

"No." Robyn kept her eyes on his, her glance never wavering, despite the personal nature of the inquiry. She wet her lips. "Have you?"

Nick felt himself growing hard. Again. "No."

Robyn smiled softly and kept looking at his face. Obviously, Nick thought, she was as curious about him as he was about her. "Are you ever going to get married?" he asked.

Several heartbeats passed. Robyn finally dropped her gaze. She uncrossed her legs, then crossed them again in the opposite direction. "If I find the love of my life," she stipulated.

Nick watched as she tugged her skirt down toward her knees. What he wouldn't give to be on the other side of the room, where the view of her legs was bound to be better, instead of right beside her. With effort, he resisted the urge to cover one of her hands with his. "What if you hit forty and still haven't found him?"

Robyn shrugged, the involuntary movement once again drawing his eyes to her breasts. "Then I won't marry," she said.

Now that would be a shame, Nick thought. A woman like Robyn shouldn't have to go through life alone. "How come?" he asked, even though he had never been one to want, or even seriously think about, marriage.

Robyn's mouth tightened into a thin line. She stared ahead. The film had stopped rewinding, but like him, she made no move to start it.

"Because I'd rather be alone, with the chance of meeting the one man in this entire universe who is absolutely perfect for me, than spend my life with someone who's not right," she said finally.

Nick regarded her admiringly. "You're a tough customer."

"Practical," Robyn corrected with a heartfelt sigh. She picked up the remote control and shifted it from palm to palm. "Maybe because I've seen what happens to someone who marries someone they don't really love."

"And who might this someone be?"

She looked at him, her mouth curling in a half smile, her eyes testing him. "You really want to know?"

"I really want to know."

"It was my older sister. She married this guy not because she loved him but because he was extremely smart and ambitious and she thought he would be a good provider."

"Is she still married?"

"Oh, yes. She's got two kids, tons of clothes, a fabulous house, three cars, one of which is a Mercedes, a swimming pool, and a vacation home in the Rockies. And she looks ten years older than she is."

"You sound sad for her."

Robyn's lips twisted pensively. "I am. I think she's missing the greatest adventure life has to offer a person, by settling for stability rather than shooting for the ultimate in wish fulfillment."

"Which is?"

"Love with Mr. Right."

Nick's gut twisted as he thought about where love with "Mr. Right," aka Leland Kincaid, had gotten his vulnerable, recently widowed mother.

Maybe Robyn's sister was right. Maybe it was better to walk into a situation with your eyes wide open rather than with your heart worn on your sleeve. "Maybe your sister knows what she's doing," he said quietly.

"You wouldn't say that if you saw her," Robyn swore heatedly. She twisted restlessly in her seat, then turned toward him earnestly. Her mouth set stubbornly, Robyn continued in a low voice that reverberated with passion, "Besides, I think true love is worth the risk of any later heartache."

Nick thought of his mother. Cassandra thought she was in love with Leland. And Leland wanted him out of the way. If not for his mother's infatuation with Leland, I wouldn't be in this situation, Nick thought. And ten to one, neither would Robyn.

Nick shook his head firmly. "I think you're wrong about that, sweetheart. I think romantic love is just an excuse for people to act crazy and irresponsible and not be held accountable for their actions."

"You're thinking about your mother now, aren't you?"

Nick nodded. "The simple fact of the matter is, Robyn, that she married much too quickly after my father's death."

Robyn's expression turned troubled. "Don't you want her to be happy?"

"Sure, I do. I just don't think Leland can do that for her. In fact, in the short time they've been married, he's done nothing but tear our family apart and alienate me from my mother."

Robyn was silent, thinking, Nick guessed, about whatever she'd been told. "Are you sure you haven't done that all by yourself?" Robyn asked. "I mean, have you stopped to consider the fact that Leland is good for Cassandra? After all, he did step in to run Wyatt & Company when it became too much for her to handle. I know for myself he's put in very long hours, and yet he's been available to your mother, night and day, whenever and however she needed him. If it was a society ball, he was there. If it was a business calamity—and trust me we've had a few—he was there."

"Leland stepped in for only one reason," Nick interjected grimly. Robyn might have been bamboozled, same as his mother, but he wasn't about to be. "He wants my mother's money."

Robyn's spine stiffened. "Leland is already rich. He doesn't need your mother's money."

How Nick wished that was true. But he knew even if Robyn didn't, it just wasn't so. "For some people, Robyn, there is no limit to greed."

Chapter Six

"I'm disappointed in you, Nick." Robyn's soft, sexy voice interrupted the silence. Nick glanced up inquiringly. "I thought you would enjoy seeing the sunset," she said.

Normally, Nick thought, he *would* enjoy seeing the sunset. God knows, it had been a spectacular one. "My mind is on other things," he said gruffly, ignoring the faint sheen of hurt and resentment in her eyes.

There was no doubt Robyn had gone to a lot of trouble arranging the meal, just as she had tried hard this afternoon to entertain him with some movies. The table had been dragged out onto the patio of Nick's third-floor room and set with snowy-white linen, fine china and crystal. Two long-stemmed candles were their only light. If not for the bulky form of Joseito, ensconced just a few feet away, his gun holstered at his side, and the constant intrusions of Carlos, the cook, it would have been quite a romantic evening indeed.

"Look, Nick." Robyn sighed. "I know this isn't exactly how you envisioned spending your week. I know you're upset because your mother hasn't called us back yet—"

"Tell me about it!" Nick grumbled with real feeling.

"But I can't keep apologizing for the inconvenience," Robyn continued pragmatically.

"You probably wouldn't have to if you kept the phone cords attached all the time, instead of having Joseito lock them up in the safe."

Robyn frowned. "You know why I can't do that."

"Don't trust me?"

"Besides, I've had Joseito attach the cords so that your mother can get through."

Nick grimaced. The village idiot could see the holes in this plan. "Suppose she's delayed?"

Robyn frowned. "I admit, it's hardly a foolproof system, Nick—"

"Look," Nick interrupted, the last of his patience dwindling fast. "All I want from you is for you to let me call my mother now and explain why I wasn't at our meeting last night."

Abruptly, Robyn's face changed, becoming almost a mask of distrust. Why, Nick had no idea. It couldn't still be the tabloid photo, could it? He had told her how he'd happened to end up in bed with those women. More likely it was the threats he'd made against his conniving stepfather. Exasperation flowed through him in tidal waves. Nick clenched his fists. He should have known better than to state his goals so clearly. He'd wanted to deal honestly and openly with the situation, but Leland had turned his usual forth-rightness against him with Robyn.

Unable to help himself, Nick ground out, "Dammit, Robyn, what do I have to say or do to make you understand that it is imperative for me to talk to my mother? Now!"

"I told you Leland said she'd call as soon as she could!"

"Well, she hasn't!" Nick had been played with long enough.

"She will!"

"And in the meantime, I'm just supposed to sit here and wait?"

"Yes. That's the plan. Though you might try eating, if you want to help yourself feel better and pass the time."

Nick's teeth clenched. Only the shadow of Joseito's powerful form kept him from reaching across the table, grabbing Robyn by the arms, and hauling her out of her seat.

Gritting his teeth together, he began again. Maybe if Robyn just understood how important this was, maybe if he gave her a little more information, she would be inclined to help him. "Listen, Robyn, this is more than a social call we're talking about. My mother must be worried sick!"

"Why? She knows I would never hurt you."

You already have, Robyn. By taking sides against me.

Wetting his lips, Nick reined in his temper and tried again. "I've got to persuade her to rescind the power of attorney she gave to Leland and give me control of the company instead."

Robyn's eyes widened as she stared at him, aghast. Then, just as swiftly, they narrowed knowingly. Idly she fingered the gold-leaf rim of her plate. "There's just one tiny problem with that picture, Nick," she said sweetly.

"What?"

She looked up at him defiantly. Her sable hair framed her heart-shaped face and flowed in loose thick waves past her shoulders. "I don't want you to get control of Wyatt & Company."

For one long moment, Nick felt as if he'd been sucker-punched in the gut. He spared a quick glance at a grim-faced Joseito, then turned the full force of his frustration on Robyn. "Why the hell not?" he demanded angrily.

"All right, I'll tell you." Robyn put her fork down with more-than-necessary force. "For starters, let's talk about the telegram you sent Leland, warning him you'd get the power of attorney back no matter what it took."

Nick's glance narrowed. He had expected that to remain private family business. "How'd you know about that?"

Robyn glanced at him reprovingly. "At least you're not denying it."

"Why would I?" He thumped the center of his chest with the flat of his palm. "I've made no secret of the fact that I think my mother made a huge mistake marrying that man."

Robyn's glance became as distant as her tone. "I can't speak to that, Nick."

"You're damn straight you can't!" Nick snapped. This wasn't her family, it was his, and he was the only one qualified to judge whether what was going on was proper or improper.

"But I can help prevent you from using Wyatt & Company as a weapon in this quarrel you have with your new stepfather," she continued.

Nick studied her upturned nose and long-lashed sable-brown eyes, then glowered a warning. If she knew what was best for her, she'd stay out of his private affairs. He leaned in closer. "Why do you care?"

Robyn rested both elbows on the table, steepled her fingers together and glared back at him. "Because I love Wyatt & Company and I don't want to lose my job!"

Nick leaned back away from her and took a sip of wine. Damn, but she was as pretty tonight as she was aggravating. Especially in that silky-looking sleeveless pink shirtdress, with the wide alligator belt and the row of buttons down the front. Buttons that started midbreast and stopped being fastened at midthigh. It was a simple enough design, with its formfitting bodice and full pleated skirt. And yet it was sexy as hell, maybe because it showed the delectable softness of her shoulders, more than a hint of cleavage, and quite a bit of two very slim, very sexy legs.

"Who says I'd fire you?" he asked.

"Whether or not you'd keep me on is not what's at issue here, Nick," Robyn retorted hotly, vaulting to her feet. She strode over to the walled terrace and stood looking out at the night.

Nick followed her to the wall, his steps as slow as hers had been hurried. He touched her cheek with the back of his hand. "Then what is?"

She rounded on him just as Joseito lumbered to his feet and stepped back to break the contact. "You couldn't care less about fashion. You've said so yourself."

Nick pivoted so closely to her, she was forced to turn, too, to avoid being run over. When he had her where he wanted her—with her back against the balcony wall—he braced his legs apart, folded his arms against his chest and continued their conversation. "So?"

Robyn held out a hand, stop-sign fashion, both to keep Joseito from interfering, and to indicate that he should leave the room. Then she tipped up her head and let out a wavering breath. "So, under your lackadaisical, laissez-faire leadership, the company would falter in no time, Nick."

"You're sure about that?" he asked, eyes gleaming.

Robyn's glance hardened as she tipped her chin up another defiant notch. "I know this—it takes only one bad season or two to lose market share. And when that happens—" she made a dusting-off motion with both hands "—you may as well forget it."

"Did Leland tell you that?"

"No," Robyn countered stiffly. Her pretty chin lifted. "Your father did."

Nick studied her with growing fascination. It amazed him that she could be so loyal, not just to his father, who had deserved her devotion, but to someone like Leland, who didn't. "Let's just say, for argument's sake, that I buy that sales philosophy—" he began.

"You should," Robyn interrupted heatedly. "It's the truth!"

"What else is in this for you?" Nick demanded.

Robyn stared at him, clearly as aggravated with him as he was with her. "What do you mean?"

"I mean you must stand to gain something here," Nick said logically. "Otherwise, I just can't see you putting your own future in jeopardy by agreeing to help shanghai me across the border. So what is it?" he probed, pushing her to the limit. "Has he offered you money?"

Robyn avoided his eyes and crossed her arms at her waist. "No, not exactly."

This was going to be like pulling teeth. "Then what?" Nick grated irritably. "A promotion? Perks? A golden parachute? A town home on Turtle Creek? *What, Robyn?*"

She sidled past him and marched several paces away, then pivoted to face him, threw back her shoulders and lifted her chin a haughty notch. "If you must know, I'm in line for a promotion I've worked damn hard for." She paused briefly, for the first time looking just a tad uncomfortable with the situation. "My getting it depends on my ability to think on my feet and handle sticky situations."

Nick quirked a brow. "Like my unexpected, un-wanted return to Dallas?"

To Nick's surprise, Robyn did not react to his sardonic tone. Her expression remained cool and pragmatic. "Exactly."

Nick stepped closer, and wished he hadn't. All he could smell was the sexy, flowery scent of her skin and hair. All he could see was her upturned face, the softness of her parted lips, and the luminous sheen in her sable brown eyes. Once again, he wished he could forget, even for a moment, the conflict that stood between them and simply take her into his arms. He wanted to kiss her until she swooned, and judging by that sexy dress she was wearing, not to mention the one she'd worn earlier in the day, he had to wonder if that wasn't exactly what Robyn and Leland were depending on—despite Robyn's coy act. "Did your assignment include seducing me?" he asked, his voice dropping a husky notch.

As the insult sank in, color rose in her cheeks until it was twice the pink of her dress. "No." Robyn pushed the words through her teeth. "I would never have agreed to that."

Nick wanted to believe her. The facts told him otherwise. "But you could be bought," he countered with a lightness that did nothing to lessen the shattering accusation of his words.

A plea for compassion pooled in her eyes. Softly she said, "I know on the surface it sounds crazy, but the truth is I only want what is good for the company, Nick."

Looking into her eyes, he could almost believe her. "And I only want what is best for my mother," Nick said coolly.

Robyn went back to the table set for two and sat down, then waited for him to follow suit. "And what is best for your mother, Nick?" Robyn asked as Carlos appeared. He cleared away their dinner plates and brought out their dessert.

"Dumping this jerk Leland as quickly as possible."

"What about the company?" Robyn asked.

"Why do you care about the company?" Nick retorted.

"Because I don't want to lose everything I have worked for the past ten years. Because I don't want to start over anywhere else, especially not now."

Nick understood that. He even applauded her honesty and forthrightness about her own ambition. But none of that changed his own feelings about what course he needed to take for his happiness and peace of mind. "The company comes a very distant second," he said, and watched her face fall. "It's my family I'm worried about here, Robyn. It's my family that comes first."

NICK WOKE to the sun streaming in through the windows. For a moment, he was disoriented. Then, from the lack of sheets on the bed and his loose-fitting clothing, he realized exactly where he was.

Hauling himself over the side of the bed, he rubbed a hand wearily across his face. He hadn't expected to fall that deeply asleep last night. The ordeal, and his thwarted efforts to contact his mother, must have been getting to him.

Rising, he strode soundlessly to the open French windows and slipped through them. He glanced down and saw Robyn on the patio below. She was seated in a chaise, her knees bent, her feet flat on the cushion beneath her. Clad only in a tiny tropical-print bikini, she had a sketch pad propped against her knees and was busily sketching.

She looked up, smiled and waved as if it were any normal day. "Hey, you're up."

"No joke, amigo," Nick replied bad temperedly as he rubbed his hand over the sandpaper roughness of his jaw.

"I'll be right up."

She was as good as her word, only she wasn't clad simply in the figure-revealing bikini, Nick noted with disappointment, but a knee-length cover-up, as well. Unfortunately for him, though, the cover-up was so sheer as to be provocative rather than modest. And he wasn't the only one who'd noticed, Nick thought, as Carlos followed Robyn into the room.

Carlos set the breakfast tray he was carrying down on the table and turned to Robyn. "Is there anything else, *señorita?*"

"This is fine, Carlos. Thank you. I'm sure Nick will enjoy his breakfast as much I enjoyed mine."

Carlos smiled at Robyn shyly and backed out of the door.

"Another admirer?" Nick asked grumpily.

Robyn sent him an innocent look. "What do you mean?"

Nick sauntered over to where she leaned against the wall. He propped his hands on either side of her and leaned over her. Eyes glittering, he raked a hot glance down the length of her before slowly returning to her eyes. Sure from the new pink in her cheeks that he'd caught her attention, he drawled, "Joseito's little brother. The small guy in the white cook's uniform who was just in here, drooling—"

"Drooling!" Robyn repeated, aghast. She flattened herself against the wall. "Honestly, Nick—"

If there was anything Nick wasn't interested in, it was outraged feminine protestations. Eyes narrowed, he leaned in a little closer, until his chest was a mere half inch from hers. "Do you really think you should be cavorting around half-naked in front of any of us?"

Palm flat against his chest, Robyn gave him a shove, then used his momentary imbalance to slip beneath his arm. Striding a safe distance away, she retorted, "First of all, it is not my fault you spied on me from up above and saw me in my bikini."

"Isn't it?" Nick interrupted with a skeptical glance.

Her breasts heaving above the low-cut top, Robyn replied, "I was sunbathing in private, Nick. Second," she said, making a sweeping motion that encompassed her from shoulder to thigh, "I have a cover-up on that reaches from my neck to my knees. I'm hardly half-naked."

"That's a matter of opinion," Nick drawled as his glance roved over her nicely rounded form visible beneath the white mesh cover-up. He'd never seen a more perfect pair of breasts, such a tiny waist, or long lissome legs....

"I don't see how," Robyn retorted right back.

Nick sensed Robyn was the kind of woman who would take a mile if given an inch. Hands on her shoulders, he propelled her to the full-length mirror. "Take a look at yourself. Look at your hair." He fingered some of the thick sable strands, watching as they slid like silk through his fingers. "See how deliciously messy it is?" He touched her cheek with the back of his palm. "Now look at your face. See how your nose and cheeks and even lips are flushed with sun?" His voice dropped a mesmerizing notch. "Look lower, to the open vee of your cover-up. See how when you move, even in the slightest, how the gauzy white fabric molds to your breasts and tummy and thighs? I can see everything you've got through that thing, honey, and you've got a lot."

Robyn jerked out of his grasp. Her cheeks were flaming from outrage.

Instead of the tongue-lashing he expected, however, she snapped out coldly, "Watch yourself, Nick. You sound jealous."

I *am* jealous, he thought, stunned, then sauntered after her, just as coolly. "I'm thinking of your well-being, Robyn. It'd be smarter to stay dressed."

Robyn tossed her mane of hair. "No one here has any trouble containing their animal instincts except you."

"Right." Nick rolled his eyes in exasperation. "You're telling me you haven't noticed the goo-goo eyes Carlos makes every time he's within three feet of you, or the way Joseito comes on like a combination big brother and father to you?"

"They're nice men. Both of them. And as for Carlos making goo-goo eyes at me—" Robyn glared at him heatedly. "You're imagining it!"

"Oh, really?" Nick asked. It infuriated him when people wouldn't open their eyes and see what was really going on around them, but instead, insisted on leaving their blinders on. "Tell me, Robyn. Am I imagining this?" He yanked her into his arms and covered her mouth with a searing, breath-stealing kiss. There was a second's fight in her, fierce, impassioned, and then she went limp against him. Her arms reached up to wrap around his shoulders. Instead of pushing him away, she was holding him close, curving those soft warm breasts into the hard length of him, and kissing him back with an intensity that went straight to his soul.

Then, when he had capitulated to her, every bit as much as she had surrendered herself to him, Robyn suddenly put both hands on his chest and shoved. "Dammit, Nick," she panted as she came to her senses. "Behave!"

Behave? Impossible, Nick thought. When he was around Robyn. When she looked as beautiful as she did. When she practically dared him to kiss her, then melted in his arms the moment he did. Behave? The only way he'd be able to behave was if behaving meant taking her into his bed, holding her close, and making fierce, passionate love to her all day long.

"Besides," Robyn continued heatedly, "this latest ploy of yours is not going to work."

"What ploy?" Nick blinked. He hadn't the slightest idea what she was talking about.

"You know very well what ploy," Robyn informed him haughtily. "You're trying to seduce me into helping you, now that your efforts to talk me into it have failed. Well, it's not going to work!"

"I never said it was!" Nick thundered back irately. "And that wasn't what I was doing!"

"Oh, no?" Robyn's eyes narrowed. "Then what was that kiss all about?" she asked coolly.

What, indeed? Nick swore. It couldn't be . . . could it?

"Nick . . . ?" Robyn asked cautiously, as he felt the blood drain from his face. "Are you all right?"

Nick gritted his teeth, hoping his initial assessment of his feelings was as wrong as he wanted it to be. "Sure I'm all right." He smiled, giving lie to any hopes either of them might have had that his feelings for her could possibly be genuine. "And you're right," Nick said, holding his desire for her in check. He lifted an apologetic glance to her and confessed, "I was sounding like a jealous suitor."

"And then some," Robyn agreed breathlessly. Her eyes remained serious, concerned.

"But then maybe that's to be expected," Nick continued casually.

Robyn looked lost. "What are you talking about?" she said slowly, still studying his face for even the minutest change.

Nick lifted a hand to the back of his neck and massaged the tenseness out of the muscles there. He might as well level with Robyn. Their situation was complicated enough, without the two of them making it any crazier by adding physical and emotional dependence to the mix.

"Surely you've heard of the Stockholm Syndrome—where the captive first becomes dependent upon his or her kidnapper for survival, then confuses that feeling, the fierce drive to survive, for love?" He had studied it briefly in college, and read about it happening to others. But never had Nick imagined, not in his wildest dreams, that this could ever happen to him, even if he were to be kidnapped.

Robyn's face turned ashen. She clenched both hands together in front of her. "You don't think..." She swallowed hard and turned another shade paler. "Nick, that isn't happening here."

"You're right," Nick agreed readily. He was in charge of this situation, and his feelings. "It isn't happening," Nick said flatly, "if for no other reason than it would go against everything I believe in." He had never been much for romance, anyway. He sure as hell didn't want to embark upon a traumatic, stress-induced romance that would fade at the first hint of reality creeping in. If and when he ever gave his heart to anyone, he wanted it to be forever. He grasped her arms and looked down at her sternly. "I never play the romantic fool, Robyn. Not for my stepfather. Not for you. As for the kiss…" He shrugged and released the light grasp he held on her arms, telling himself the more distance he put between himself and Robyn, the better. "The kiss is the risk you run if you're going to stand guard over me night and day." And maybe if she knew that, he reasoned, she'd do a better job of both covering up and keeping her distance.

"Like hell it is, Nick Wyatt!" Robyn shot back.

Nick grinned, enjoying the flare of anger in her eyes. Just for the heck of it, he shrugged his shoulders indolently and pushed her a little more. "I have to do something with my time."

"Then try knitting," Robyn stormed, looking very much as if she wanted to deck him then and there. "Because you won't put your hands on me again!"

"LELAND, I THOUGHT you said Cassandra was going to call," Robyn began half an hour later, when she finally caught up with Leland at the office.

"She tried twice last night, but the lines between here and there were down somewhere." Leland breathed an audible sigh of relief. "I'm glad to know they are okay now. I was beginning to get worried when we couldn't get through to you at the prearranged time."

So was I, Robyn thought, even as niggling doubt crept in and made her question the credibility of Leland's story. Maybe the best thing to do was forget last night and move on. "Can I talk to her now?"

"She's at a charity luncheon this afternoon."

"Is she coming back to the office?"

"I'm not sure. She expected to be tied up for quite a while. The benefit's for AIDS research. You know that's a pet cause of hers."

Robyn sighed. There was no question that was a worthy cause, and one that had been well publicized in advance. She had known about this luncheon for weeks and probably would have taken the afternoon off and attended herself had she been in Dallas. There was no reason for her to doubt Leland just because Nick resented him for marrying his mother. "Well, when can I talk to her then?" Robyn asked.

"This evening. I promise. I'll have her call." Leland paused. "What's wrong? Nick hasn't freed himself, has he?"

I only wish, Robyn thought as she recalled Nick's kiss, and her passionate response. She had kissed her fair share of men over the years, but never had she kissed anyone the way she had Nick. Could it be possible, she wondered, horrified by the thought, that Nick was right, that this attraction they felt for each other was some sort of weird offshoot of the kidnapping itself? No, she thought, I'm smarter than that. Giving her heart over to a man like Nick would mean putting her heart in jeopardy.

"Just tell me what's wrong," Leland continued to prod.

Robyn sighed. "It's Nick. He's getting out of control."

"What do you mean?"

I mean he's kissing me like there's no tomorrow! Robyn thought. Worse, I find myself liking it.

"Just . . . restless. Demanding," Robyn fibbed, too embarrassed about what had happened between them to tell the truth.

"What does he want?"

"To see his mother ASAP."

"That," Leland said flatly, "will never happen. Cassandra is still far too furious with him. She wants him in Mexico, Robyn, until she's calm enough to deal with him."

"When will that be?"

"I'm not sure. A few more days. The end of the week."

Robyn drew a wavering breath. "That's a long time for us to be cooped up here together, Leland."

"Now, now, Robyn," Leland soothed, sounding more like a father than a boss. "Just calm down and think this through. Think of what we all have to gain if we can keep Nick out of sight for a few more days. Think about what you'll be doing for the company. Think of all the jobs you'll be saving if we don't have to close down the Young Juniors line, but can let you infuse new life into it and expand it, instead. I know you're a clever young woman. I know you can handle Nick, if you just put your mind to it."

Could she? Robyn sighed. "He isn't cooperating at all," she reported. Which gave her reason to suspect that perhaps Nick wasn't the reckless irresponsible playboy Leland had made him out to be after all.

"He hasn't made another escape attempt, has he?"

"No, but we've given him no opportunity. We took away everything he could possibly use to make a rope."

"Still, he could have been rough with you if he really wanted to get away, couldn't he? He could have beaten you up or tried to take you as a hostage. Actually, when you come right down to it, Robyn, if Nick had really wanted to get away, he could have knocked you out cold and then tied you up and taken off."

Had Leland knowingly put her in danger? Robyn wondered, as chills ran down her spine.

"But he didn't. And you know why?" Leland continued persuasively. "Because at heart Nick isn't that kind of man. He's not cruel or vicious or violent. Just a little hot tempered and reckless. Passionate. Promiscuous."

Robyn thought of the picture of Nick in bed with those four near-naked women. He claimed that had been forced on him, too, but he hadn't looked as if he were suffering when the photo was snapped. Instead, he'd had a goofy grin on his face, even as he'd unsuccessfully tried to hide his eyes from the camera with the back of his hand. "I guess you're right. He could have been a lot more violent in his resistance of the kidnapping," Robyn said thoughtfully.

"But he hasn't been."

"No, he hasn't."

"Then that just proves my point," Leland soothed. "Nick might be behaving as if he's chafing at the restraints you've put upon him, but in reality he's not as anxious to leave as he would like you to think. In fact, he's probably secretly getting quite a kick out of the whole thing. After all, how often does any man get to be shanghaied off to paradise by a beautiful woman?"

Not often, Robyn knew. In fact, for most men, it was never. Nick had seemed to be enjoying their kisses, Robyn thought. But he wasn't enjoying being cooped up.

"You said he would relax and enjoy this," she accused softly. "That once he was here, he would say what the hell and just take the unexpected vacation."

"And he will, Robyn, my dear, he will," Leland persisted, seemingly as firm in his beliefs as she was anxious. "All you have to do is be a little more charming. A little more feminine and beguiling."

Cold chills raced up and down her spine as Robyn tried to interpret exactly what that meant. "Leland. You're not—" Robyn paused and bit her lip. "You're not expecting me to sleep with him, are you?" Surely that wasn't in the deal!

There was a long, tense silence, followed by Leland's hearty, "No, no, of course not, dear! Just lead him on a merry chase! Nick always was the sort who liked to chase his women a while before he caught them! So you concentrate on that—forget about letting him actually catch you—and leave the rest to me. I promise you, when you return at the end of the week

you'll have everything you've worked for, everything
you've wanted.''

"I hope so," Robyn murmured. Already it was beginning to seem that she had paid far too high a price
for her success.

Chapter Seven

"You can go now, Joseito," Robyn said several hours later, as she paused beside Nick's door.

Nick turned to look at her through the open portal. Robyn was a vision in a pink floral drop-shouldered sundress with a tight bodice and a flared skirt. She'd pinned one side of her hair back away from her face with a white gardenia plucked from the bushes below. Her legs were tanned the same rich gold as her arms, face and shoulders. They were also silky smooth and bare of stockings. Her feet were encased in delicate white sandals. She looked festive and pretty enough to go to a garden party, which irritated the hell out of him. He was in no mood to celebrate at all.

"I'll take over for the next couple of hours and keep an eye on Nick," Robyn continued with a breezy smile.

"Thanks." Joseito stood stiffly, as if he were as tired of playing guard as Nick was of being guarded. He reached for the door and closed them in. The lock turned, sounding like a death knell to Nick.

This day was not turning out to be any better than the previous one. He'd spent the morning showering, playing solitaire, pacing the room repeatedly, and waiting for a phone call from his mother that never came. His mood was foul. It didn't help any to realize Robyn and Joseito still thought they had to baby-sit him every moment, when he had decided hours before to stay until he found out what Leland was really up to. Keeping his eyes on her face, Nick sauntered toward Robyn, taunting, "Still don't trust me, hmm?"

Recalling her promise to Leland to charm Nick, and hence help him enjoy his unexpected stay in Mexico, Robyn pointedly ignored his barb and said in the most cheerful voice she could muster, "I thought you'd like company for your noon meal."

"What I'd like is to speak with my mother."

"I've told you that will happen," Robyn promised.

"When?"

"Tonight."

"You said last night or this morning—"

"The phones were down last night."

Yeah, Nick thought, right. Robyn was putting him off. "What about this morning?" he snapped.

"This morning, and this afternoon, your mother is attending a benefit luncheon for charity."

So what was new about that? Cassandra had always been active in Dallas charities. Since his father's death, her activities had only escalated.

"I know she'll call," Robyn reiterated.

"She said that?"

"To Leland," Robyn confirmed agreeably, "who told me."

He stared straight ahead. "So you haven't talked to her then."

"No."

"It figures." Nick ground his right fist into his left palm and swore heatedly beneath his breath. "That damn Leland has her so isolated."

Not that Robyn could see. From Robyn's vantage point, Leland seemed to keep his new wife apprised of everything down to the minutest detail. He included her in all the top-level meetings and decision-making. In fact, the department heads were constantly generating reports and summaries for Cassandra's perusal. "Look, Nick, I'm sorry your mother hasn't called. I'd like to talk to her, too. But given the depth of her involvement in her charity work, and the complexity of our... situation, it's not surprising to me that she put off returning the call."

"You really believe that?" Nick sent her a sharply disapproving glance.

Robyn drew herself up to her full five feet nine inches. "I have no reason to distrust your mother."

"What about Leland?"

She blinked. "What?"

Nick leaned over her, so they were standing toe-to-toe, nose to nose. "Are you telling me you'd trust him with your life?" he demanded.

Robyn paled. And even though she tried to hide it, Nick could see she was struggling with her answer, that she was beginning at last to have doubts about Nick's slimy but charming stepfather.

"Leland's given me no reason to distrust him," she said stiffly, hugging her crossed arms to her chest.

Nick's disapproving glare deepened. "What do you call his getting you into this mess?" he asked with exaggerated patience.

Robyn's sable eyes sparked to life. Uncrossing one of her arms, she waved an accusing finger under his nose. "*You* got us into this mess, Nick. With your threats and your shenanigans and your disinterest in your family's business. Leland is trying to save us."

Save himself, you mean, Nick thought grimly, but he didn't say it. Now was not the time for arguing with Robyn. Instead, he merely wanted to further her doubts. He stepped so close his breath stirred her hair, then lowered his voice another persuasive notch. "Come on, Robyn, be honest now," he murmured, lightly grasping her arm. "Don't you find any of this the least bit suspicious? Not even my kidnapping?"

Robyn pulled away from him. "Getting you out of town as quickly and quietly as possible was what your mother wanted, Nick."

Nick wished he could say that wasn't so with complete conviction, that his mother never would have had him "taken" out of town, whether he wanted to go or not. Unfortunately, the truth was that his mother had been royally ticked off at him for his au naturel appearance on the cover of *Naughty Not Nice*. So ticked off that some small doubting part of him was really afraid that with enough diligent effort on Leland's part, enough misrepresentation of Nick's actions, that his mother really might think the worst of him. And if she did, all was lost anyway, because she would never let him have control of the company, not at her new husband's expense, not now when Nick was the brunt of so many tacky jokes.

He swallowed hard. Speculating on the worst wasn't going to help. He had to think about the best-case scenario here, not the worst. And the best-case scenario was his mother not only forgiving him, but also listening to him when he told her that he had been set up, probably by her greedy new husband. Now all he had to do was convince Robyn of that.

"Getting me out of Dallas was what Leland wanted, too," Nick said heavily. "And it was more to his benefit than my mother's—who, by the way, seems more likely to tell me to get the hell out of Dallas than to force me from it at gunpoint."

His words hit home. Nick could see it in Robyn's face. Despite her cool bravado, she was beginning to have doubts about Leland's story, too. Real doubts. And that meant his plan to sway her to his side was working. The question was, could it work fast enough?

This is a difficult assignment Cassandra and I are giving you, Robyn, but one we feel sure you are up to, Leland had told her. *But beware. Nick will do anything to get his way. He's quite the successful womanizer. Maybe because he always seems to figure out what women want him to say.*

And in this case, Robyn thought, what she wanted Nick to say was that he was innocent of all wrongdoing. That she wasn't wrong to be having these ardent thoughts about him, that she wasn't wrong to suddenly be feeling almost more sympathy for him than she could manage.

Nick was still watching her, waiting. Testing and calculating her response. Robyn drew a slow breath. She raked a hand through her hair. "Look," she said, "I can see you're in no mood for company for lunch—" She wanted nothing more than to get out of there.

"The hell I'm not!" Nick said. Robyn glanced up sharply. "I'm dying for some company. Yours in particular," he said.

Under any other circumstances, Robyn would have taken his words as the highest compliment. Certainly her feminine ego was flattered. It pleased her to know she appealed to a man as handsome and virile as Nick. But his words also signaled a warning. Leland had told her Nick might try to seduce her into siding with him. In fact, Leland had said that was usually Nick's first tactic when it came to getting what he wanted from women.

"Come on, Robyn," Nick said softly. Again he touched her arm, imploringly this time. His eyes meshed with hers. "Don't go. At least not yet. I'd like you to join me."

Robyn hesitated. She had promised Joseito she'd keep an eye on Nick.

"And," Nick continued with a charming smile that lit up his utterly masculine features in a warm and welcoming way, "if it's not too much trouble to feed me somewhere else in this villa, I'd like to do that, too."

Robyn understood his cooped-up feeling. Although just thirty-six hours had passed since they'd arrived here, she was beginning to feel cooped up, too. And she had the run of the entire place! Nick had spent almost all his time in this room or the terrace beyond. "How about the formal dining room?" she suggested.

Nick sent a yearning glance at the open windows. It was a beautiful day. Sunny, breezy and warm. "If it's all the same to you, I'd rather be outside."

So you can try to make another escape? Robyn wondered. Studying Nick's reaction closely in an effort to figure out his intent, she slid her hands into the pockets of her sundress and suggested amiably, "How about the terrace off my room?"

Nick looked only half-amenable to that. "How about the terrace on the first floor?" he countered.

The first floor, with its proximity to the beach, and the road, was just too risky. "My room, Nick," Robyn said quietly, still watching his face. "Take it or leave it."

"Okay." Nick sighed, giving in with grace. "Your room."

With Joseito accompanying them, they went down to Robyn's room. Nick glanced around curiously as they moved through the surroundings, taking in everything from the neat way she'd stacked her cosmetics to the sketch pad open on the bed.

Curious enough to momentarily forget his manners, he bent down to pick it up and glanced at the colorful Mexican dress she had designed. "Is this what you were working on this morning?"

Robyn nodded. She gave him a long, considering gaze, daring him to make a rude remark. "It's for my first collection of resort wear," she said.

Nick had realized she was a talented seamstress, by the swift, efficient way she had altered his clothes. But the dress in front of him was no run-of-the-mill, off-the-rack design and they both knew it. He regarded her with respect, one professional to another. "It's very pretty," he murmured appreciatively. *Like you.*

They might be in different professions, but he still knew quality when he saw it, and everything about this dress Robyn had designed spoke of quality. Quality and fresh, original talent.

Robyn smiled, tapping the page. "But is it practical?"

Practical? Nick thought. What had ever been practical about a woman in a dress! Dresses were for enticing men...showing off breasts, and waists and long, silky legs....

Nick forced himself to stop digressing. Why women wore dresses was of no concern to him. He was a race-car driver, not a clothier. Just as it was no concern of his why Robyn had dressed up for their lunch. Swallowing hard, he turned his glance back to her sketch.

"Well, Nick," Robyn prodded, enjoying his discomfiture, "is it practical?"

Nick hadn't the faintest idea what made a dress practical. So he did what he always did when called upon to render an opinion on women's fashion: he guessed. "I think so," he said firmly. After all, it was the kind of dress all sorts of women could wear.

Robyn planted both hands on her slender hips and studied him keenly, as if she were testing his knowledge of the clothing industry. "Why do you say that?" she pressed, her sable eyes direct.

Again Nick had to force his eyes away from her face, away from her soft mouth and pert nose and intelligent eyes, and back to the sketch. Practical, practical, he thought. Why the hell was this thing practical? Only one thing came immediately to mind. Rather than hem and haw around all afternoon, he went with it. "See the elastic neck and sleeves?" he pointed out with sudden inspiration as his fingertip traced the colored markings of her pen. "The elastic waist of the skirt?"

"Yeah?" Robyn tilted her head up to his, so her mouth was just under his.

Damn, but he wanted to kiss her. Again. Not sure he could stop if he got started, though, not if she melted against him as she had the last time, Nick paused and took a deep breath.

"What of them?" Robyn asked.

Nick smiled, swallowed and tried to quell the lusty gleam he could feel emanating from his eyes. "All that elastic instead of buttons and zippers makes the dress

you designed exceedingly easy to get off. Therefore,"
Nick announced, "the dress is highly practical. At
least from my point of view."

Robyn rolled her eyes, completely disgusted. "That
wasn't why I designed the dress that way, Nick."

"No?"

"No," she confided calmly. "I designed the dress
that way to get a better fit."

"Well, the fit isn't what a man will be thinking
about when he sees his woman in that dress." If a man
saw a woman in the off-the-shoulder dress in the
sketch, he'd be thinking exactly what Nick was thinking. He'd be wondering if she was wearing a bra. And
he'd be thinking how soft and smooth her shoulders
were. He'd be thinking what it would feel like to take
that dress off, an inch at a time, and pull her close. So
close they were touching skin to skin.

This wasn't helping, Nick thought.

Determined to get his mind out of the bedroom and
away from his recurring fantasy about having Robyn
in his bed, Nick flipped to the next page in her sketch
pad. He studied it with single-minded concentration.
"What else do you have here?" he asked gruffly.

"See for yourself," Robyn replied unabashedly.

They were silent as he looked through design after
design. He'd thought he was impressed looking at the
first dress. That was nothing to what he felt after
looking at twenty of her quickly sketched designs, all
with a sexy Southwestern or Mexican flair. "Did you
just think these up?" he asked finally, wondering what
it must be like to be so talented.

"Some," Robyn admitted. "Others were inspired by some of the clothes I saw the women selling and wearing in the village. But they're all my designs, yes."

He regarded her in amazement. "Is it easy for you to do that?"

Robyn shrugged, aware of the way his glance fell across her bare shoulders. "Sometimes. Sometimes it's not so easy, but I keep at it." *Just like I'll keep resisting my desire for you.*

"You're very talented," Nick said quietly, in a way that let her know he meant it.

Their eyes locked, held. Looking at him, Robyn knew some bridge had been crossed, and some understanding of each other gained.

Carlos came in. "Luncheon is served, *señorita.*"

Nick scowled at him, resenting the interruption.

Damn it all. Why did Carlos have to come in now, when he was just beginning to win Robyn over to his side. "What are we having?" Nick asked. He was prepared not to like it, whatever it was, if only to get rid of Carlos, and the constant intrusion of being waited on, and return to their intimate conversation.

Carlos smiled. He whipped the silver covers off the plates and announced proudly, "Beef enchiladas, refried beans, Mexican rice, and guacamole salad. We will start, of course, with the salad. Sorbet will be served between every course."

The salad alone looked great. Nick scowled. Damn. He hated to send that food back, but he had to get rid of Carlos. "I don't want it," he said flatly. And then, attempting to buy Robyn and him some more time alone, he said, "Fix me something else."

Too late, he saw it had been the wrong thing to say. Carlos was crushed. And Robyn was looking at Nick as if he were a heartless bastard. "Then what do you want, Nick?" she asked sweetly.

"A steak, I guess." Maybe Carlos would have to go to the village to get one.

Carlos smiled, trying hard to hide his disappointment. "And how would you like that cooked, Señor Nick?"

"Rare," Nick started to say, then stopped. "Well-done," he said. "Very well-done." Whatever would take the longest.

Robyn smiled at Carlos like some sort of beatific angel. "I'll have the Mexican food you've prepared, Carlos. But you needn't burden yourself, bringing it up a course at a time. Serving me all at once, at the same time as Nick, will be fine."

Carlos smiled at her, his adoration for her complete.

Jealousy twisted in Nick's gut.

Damn, Nick thought. Why hadn't he thought of that? Of course the food could be served all at one time.

Now he'd come off as a pompous, demanding ass. Just what he needed to really further the budding relationship between him and Robyn.

If she weren't so pretty. If he weren't so enamored of and distracted by her looks...

He swore again.

Robyn sent him a chilly glance.

His temper flaring, Nick sent one back at her. "Well?"

"Well what?" Robyn asked.

"Let's get it over with," he said wearily, bracing himself for the worst because she looked as if she wanted to deck him. He rested his elbows on the table. In for a penny, in for a pound. Might as well make it a full-blown lapse of manners. "Aren't you going to tell me how rude I just was?"

She smiled at him condescendingly and spread her napkin over her lap. "I suspect you know that," she said with chilly indifference. Her reproving gaze lifted and arrowed straight into his. "I also suspect it's part of the plan."

Nick blinked. Now she'd really lost him. "Plan?" he echoed.

"To be so much of a pain in the butt that I won't be able to wait to get rid of you. Save your tactics, Nick," she warned tightly, then favored him with a narrow stare. "They won't work, any more than your attempt at escape did."

Nick studied the pouty thrust of her lower lip, the defiant angle of her chin. This woman had so much emotion racked up in her she was about to explode. "You're sure of that?" he bit out, letting her know with a hard glance he was a man who could only be pushed so far.

Her eyes locked with his. "Very." She smiled at him in a cool, brittle way that sent his temper soaring another notch. "Now, how about a drink? Something to relax you." She gestured toward the pitcher of frosty margaritas Carlos had brought up with the salads.

Nick shook his head. There was no telling what might happen as the day ahead of him unfolded. He wasn't about to let his reflexes to cope be dulled in the slightest. "Nothing with alcohol," he stipulated firmly. "I'll have iced tea instead."

Robyn studied him disapprovingly, then shrugged. Nick noticed that although she'd made a show of pouring herself a drink, she hadn't touched hers, either.

"Suit yourself," Robyn said, "but I think you're awfully tense."

It was hard not to be tense, Nick thought sourly as he and Robyn dug into their salads, when all he could think about, all he'd been able to think about all day, was the sight of her, first thing this morning, in that tiny bikini.

Had she designed that herself? he wondered. God knows, the fabric had fit her like a glove, molding to the luscious curves of her breasts and the sleek, long lines of her hips.

He'd been around a lot of women in his life, many of them clad in very little, but never had a woman's looks compelled him the way Robyn's had.

Carlos returned with Robyn's plate and Nick's iced tea. He set it in front of her, along with a basket of chips and some salsa. "Your dinner will be ready directly, Señor Nick."

Carlos exited, but not before making another quick adoring glance at Robyn. A glance, Nick noted with growing disdain, that she seemed completely oblivious to. How unaware could the woman be? he wondered, as his jealousy grew and flamed.

"Mmm." Robyn sighed as she let the spicy enchilada melt on her tongue. She swallowed, looking all the while as if she were in absolute heaven, and waved her fork at him. "You don't know what you're missing here, Nick. Carlos is a superb cook."

As if he couldn't see that, Nick thought sourly.

Feeling regret that he hadn't decided to eat the Mexican food first, along with Robyn, and then order the steak, Nick merely shrugged and took a sip of his iced tea. Damned if those margaritas didn't look enticing, too, he thought.

It was time to get the conversation back on track. Time to get her back in his corner. Solidly, this time. Robyn continued to eat, a distracted, almost dreamy expression on her face.

"What are you thinking about?" he asked gently. He knew what *he* was thinking about! Getting Robyn in his bed. Beneath him. Against him. Being deep inside her.

Robyn swallowed and reached absently for her glass. "Don't you have a race coming up soon?" She took a big swallow, then choked, realizing in her distracted state she had gulped down half a margarita instead of her water.

"Not for a couple of weeks," Nick said. He watched Robyn daintily dab each corner of her mouth with a point of her linen napkin. God, she was sensual, and she didn't even know it. "I cancelled everything between now and then."

"I see."

There it was again, that little edge of judgment in her voice.

"See what?" Nick said.

Her eyes lifted to his. Nick wasn't sure if it was the alcohol she had just so hastily—and mistakenly—imbibed, or the build of tension that was provoking her into taking off the kid gloves in the careful way she treated him. But she was feeling and acting reckless, all of a sudden. Damn reckless.

And he was feeling just the tiniest bit reckless, too.

"I see why you cancelled your races for the next couple of weeks."

"Really," Nick observed, making no effort to hide the sarcastic edge to his voice.

"Really," Robyn confirmed. Her eyes gleamed accusingly. "You wanted to give yourself enough time to stir up trouble at home, maybe even wreck your mother's new marriage."

"You don't know the first thing about that," Nick interrupted hotly. She was pushing all his buttons with remarkable speed. People might not always like what he said to them, but they could count on it being honest. And that, more than anything, was the problem with him and Leland. Nick wasn't about to trust, or even pretend to trust, someone he didn't.

His gut instinct told him that Leland was up to no good. Maybe he cared about Cassandra, but Leland was also out to get whatever he could out of their union, as was evidenced by the speed with which Leland had rushed his mother into marriage and then helped himself to the top position in the family company.

Nick didn't trust Leland's plans for the company, just as he didn't trust Leland's story about his previous marriage to a prominent New York socialite ending amicably. Leland was smooth, Nick had to hand him that. But he had also probably lied about any number of things. Nick was going to catch him in the act and expose him, and he would start by taking a closer look at Leland's past, the very first chance he got. If the guy was the sleazy operator that Nick suspected, then something nefarious would turn up there, in either Leland's earlier marriage or his past professional life. Nick was sure of it.

"What are you going to do if your mother doesn't want to hear your views about her new marriage?" Robyn asked grimly.

Nick had had his fill of being presumed guilty. It hurt, knowing Robyn was as gullible as the rest. "She will when she realizes that I've discovered the truth about Leland, and can present her with facts backing up my every accusation," Nick asserted stubbornly, more sure than ever, after spending the past hour with Robyn, that it was Leland who was the villain in all this. Not Robyn, and not his mother.

Robyn set her fork down and regarded him with the patience of a saint. "Leland is trying to help your mother, Nick."

Nick's gut tightened. *"Leland,"* he corrected, just as archly, *"is after her money."*

"Leland has plenty of money on his own. He doesn't need hers."

Nick decided what the hell. He might as well have a margarita, too. At least part of one. God knows, he was so tense now it would take half a bottle of tequila to make him relax his guard in the slightest. He downed the first half of his margarita and set his perfectly chilled glass down with a thud. "For some, greed knows no bounds. I suspect that Leland is one of those." *Even if you, Robyn Rafferty, are far too naive and trusting to know it.*

Robyn's mouth set as she regarded him furiously. "You really are determined not to like him, aren't you?"

She spoke as if his mistrust of his stepfather were one of the seven deadly sins, instead of just cool common sense, given the circumstances. Nick wanted to shake her. Kiss her. Anything to get her to wake up to what was really going on here. But in the end all he had were words, and so he used them to his best advantage, stating cruelly, "And you really are determined to turn a blind eye to what's going on around you. Well, you're welcome to the mess you're making, honey. So is my mother. You all are. And it is one hell of a mess, Robyn, the money my mother stands to lose to that bastard being the least of it, I suspect."

Silence fell as they stared at each other.

Carlos rushed in, plate in hand. "Here is your steak, Señor Nick."

Nick took one look at the steak. It was charred a rich brown on the outside, perfectly done on the inside. He could tell by the way Robyn was watching him that he was supposed to praise it lavishly, thank Carlos, and then fall on it like a dying man. Which he probably would have done had he not been filled with a perverse need to shake her implacable cool. So, she thought he'd behaved like a bastard so far? Well, she hadn't seen nothin' yet.

Nick fixed Robyn with a hard look. "It's underdone."

Underdone! Robyn stared back at Nick meaningfully, like a mother trying to correct a wayward child. He might be spoiled rotten and in a foul mood because of the kidnapping, but she'd be damned if she'd let him hurt Carlos's feelings again. "It is not."

"Take it back and do it over."

"Carlos—" Robyn began.

Carlos shook his head. Though his demeanor remained impeccably polite, he looked as crushed as Robyn had feared he would be. "It is all right, *señorita*. Señor Nick is right. The steak is poorly cooked." He ducked his head humbly. "I will try again."

As soon as Carlos had left, Robyn rounded on Nick. "That was a lousy thing to do, Nick."

Yeah, Nick thought, it was. But he didn't need her telling him that. Still fuming, he stared at her and knew if he stayed a second longer he would end up kissing her. They needed to be physically involved the way Texas low-water crossings needed water after a week of torrential rains.

He shoved his chair back with a resounding scrape, and stood without looking at her face. "I've changed my mind," he announced tersely. "I don't think I want lunch after all. I want to go back to my room. Now, babe."

Robyn wadded her napkin up into a crumple ball of linen and threw it down beside her plate. She shot to her feet like a rocket. "Fine," she said. "I hope you starve."

Head held high, she led the way. She was stonily silent the whole way, though Nick could feel her anger simmering. The moment they entered his room, she started in on him again. "I can't believe you did that down there."

He spread his hands wide on either side of him. "Surprise, sweetheart, I'm capable of a lot of things." Including kissing you into damn near oblivion, Nick thought.

She looked him up and down, like examining an odious piece of trash. "Probably," she agreed flatly as she lifted a lecturing finger and pointed it at his nose. "But you and I are going to get something straight right now. You are not to hurt Carlos's feelings again. Do you understand?" Robyn strung out every syllable of her last sentence and regarded him as if he were a moron.

Nick shrugged. She wasn't the only one who could play the exaggerated patience game. "You don't want me badgering the kid for his lousy cooking? Fine. Let me out of here, give me access to a phone so I can track down my mother, and I won't."

"You know that's impossible!" Robyn chided.

"Nothing's impossible, babe."

"Stop calling me that."

He grinned at her. "Anything you say, *babe.*"

Robyn drew a deep calming breath. The man was just trying to goad her into losing control of her temper. Well, it wouldn't work. "Furthermore," she continued with icy cool, "you are to stop being a selfish, self-pitying, unreliable playboy heir—in short, a royal pain—this instant!"

To have her lecturing him on the proper behavior, when she had kidnapped him and dragged him here against his will, was the last straw. "You want to know what a royal pain is?" Nick retorted, as his anger took on a real driving force. He stomped closer. "A royal pain is being locked up in this villa night and day. A royal pain is having no real choice about anything."

Robyn backed up until she hit the wall. "Now, Nick..." she said, a little breathlessly. Perhaps she had overdone it with the lecturing bit. Surely, under the circumstances, Nick was as entitled to his bad moods as everyone else.

Nick flattened a hand on the wall on either side of her and leaned in. "Now what?"

He wasn't touching her anywhere yet, but everywhere they were almost touching—chests, tummies, thighs—heat emanated in sweet, paralyzing waves. Worse, from the intent, ardent look on Nick's face, she could tell he was feeling the heat, too.

"You...don't want to do anything you'll regret." Robyn's breath caught in her lungs.

"What makes you think I'm going to regret this?" Nick said softly. He took another step nearer, so they were touching. His hands closed over her shoulders.

Robyn could feel the implacable evidence of his desire as surely as she could feel the slow heavy beating of his heart. And see the tempting firmness of his lips poised over hers. "Let me go, Nick," she said hoarsely.

"Why should I?" Nick retorted in a soft, persuasive voice that had her tilting her head up defiantly. "You started this."

"I asked you to lunch."

"In that dress."

Robyn smiled at him weakly. Maybe she could get out of this with a joke. "You would've preferred slacks?"

"I would have preferred not to be treated like some 'selfish, self-pitying, unreliable playboy heir.'"

Robyn knew she should never have called him that. She flattened both hands against his chest and pushed hard. It was like trying to move a five-ton boulder. He wasn't even flexing his muscles and he was rock hard. All over. Pulses pounding, Robyn swore silently to herself. So much for getting out of this via force. She'd have to try the cool, haughty ice-princess route. "Let me go, Nick," she repeated again baldly, then followed that with a commanding look.

"Why?" Half of his mobile mouth slanted up into a grin. "Don't you want to see where all this will lead?" he teased as he inched in closer, one leg working between the two of hers, and pressed her flat against the wall.

"No," Robyn said.

But it was too late. One of his hands had already circled the back of her neck, the other caught both her flailing hands and held them in front of her. "And I thought you were so brave," he taunted.

Oh, God, Robyn thought. It was going to happen. He was actually going to kiss her again. She could see it in his dark green eyes, feel it in the weakening of her knees, and the soft, melting sensation in her tummy. "Nick—"

"That's it, Robyn," he murmured as he dipped his head, slanting it over hers at just the right angle. His breath meshed with hers. "Call my name. Call it over and over and over again," Nick whispered enticingly, then his mouth fastened over hers, hot and quick.

She expected no gentleness. She got none. His lips were hungry. And hard. His tongue was soft and hot and unbearably sweet. He swept the insides of her mouth, languidly at first, then with growing ardor, until she was lost in the touch, taste and feel of him, in the sound of his breath, in her own low, shuddering moan.

Robyn told herself this was crazy, even as she gave in to the compelling intensity of his desire. She should fight this. Fight him. But as his mouth continued to move expertly and evocatively over hers, she could do nothing, it seemed, but surrender. Nothing had ever prepared her for this, this incredible mind-boggling pleasure. Nothing had ever prepared her for Nick.

Delighting in his victory, in the sweet vulnerability of her response, Nick released her hands and swept them aside, so there was nothing between them except the soft cotton of her floral print sundress and the equally thin layer of his shirt. And still, he thought impatiently, anxious to know every delectable inch of her, it was too much.

Robyn moaned lower in her throat. She had never known mere kisses could make her feel this alive. Never known she could delight so in the hard feel of a man's chest pressed against hers. But she did. Her nipples burned. Her tummy tingled. Lower still, there was a mounting heat and emptiness that was almost overwhelming. An emptiness that had only one cure.

She ached to know the feel of his hands upon her flesh. So much so that it no longer mattered how or why they were together, just that they were. She'd never felt such fierce, soul-shattering desire for anyone in her life.

Robyn dug her hands into the hard width of his shoulders. "Oh, babe." Nick tore his mouth from hers and kissed the exposed column of her throat. Robyn arched into him as his fingers kneaded the base of her neck, then slipped lower, coasting down her spine. Yes, she thought, yes. The next thing she knew, the back zipper of her dress had been eased open. Cool air assaulted her skin as Nick's fingertips lovingly traced her spine.

A wildfire of sensation swept through her. Dizzy with need, with wonder, Robyn arched toward him again. His mouth pressed against hers. Gently, this time. He pushed the off-the-shoulder sleeves of her sundress further down her arm, past her elbows, then her wrists.

As impatient now as he was for further contact, Robyn worked her arms entirely free of the dress. Nick stared down at her, his mouth dry. Her breasts were every bit as beautiful as he had imagined, high and round and full. There was a strip of white across the center of her breasts. Untanned skin. Nipples that were small and dusty pink. He touched her nipples, first one then the other, rubbing them with his thumb. Immediately, they tightened into hard red crowns. Robyn's breath soughed out evenly. Her sable eyes, already glazed with desire, turned even more luminous. "Nick," she whispered.

The blood thundered through him, pooling low. Nick pressed his sex into the cradle of her legs, trying to ease the ache, but the action only intensified it. Desire thundering through him in mesmerizing waves, he flattened the hard length of his body against the softness of hers. The contact wasn't enough, not nearly, and yet it was like going home, Nick thought. It was better than going home....

Still kissing her as if he had all the time in the world, Nick gently covered her breasts with the palms of his hands. Robyn gasped softly and arched into his touch. Her breasts were raised and aching. Her thighs were trembling. She was completely at the mercy of the feelings tearing through her, the pure, almost brazen sensuality she had never even realized existed within herself. Until now, she thought. Until Nick. No matter what happens, Robyn thought, I will never ever be the same. . . .

"You're so beautiful, Robyn. So hot and soft. I could take you right now," Nick murmured against her mouth, "and not regret it for an instant."

Which was exactly what she wanted, Robyn thought as Nick's mouth found her breasts and she was overwhelmed by the heat and excitement of him once again. Flames of desire flicked through her, until the warm dampness of her breasts was matched only by the warm dampness between her thighs.

Nick groaned. Gathering the hem of her dress in his hands, he pushed it past her waist, slid a hand inside the elastic of her panties. He had to have more of her. Had to, he thought, as his palms flattened against her hips. And judging from her unbridled response to his kisses and caresses, she felt the same.

He pressed her against him tightly, letting her feel his need. An answering passion ignited within her. Robyn felt her insides turn hot, liquid, and she moaned low in her throat. No one had ever made her feel this way before, so crazy and aching with need. She thought she would die if he touched her there— and die if he didn't. She wanted him that much. Wanted to feel him inside her. Deep inside her. Now. "Nick—"

"I'm here, Robyn." He slid his fingers into the nest of curls, expertly found her center. "Right here."

"Oh—" Robyn quaked as he stroked and pleased.

"I know. It's too much, isn't it?" His own voice was husky, almost raw with a mixture of wonder and desire as he brought her to the brink.

Too much was right, Robyn thought, as the last of her sanity fled and explosions started deep inside her. And then he was inside her, just as she wanted, moving fast and hard and deep. She had no idea how long their climax lasted. Only that she was shaking like a leaf when it was over. If it weren't for Nick's arms, so tight around her, she wouldn't have been able to stand up at all.

Still bowled over by what had just happened between them, Nick bent to kiss her brow. Then amazingly, he felt her pull away. Nick stared down at her. His mouth tightened as he recognized her regret.

"Robyn..." Nick's voice was hoarse, pleading.

Her spine stiffened even more. "Don't you think you've already said and done enough for one afternoon?" Robyn demanded curtly as she slipped her arms into the drop sleeves of her dress and tugged the bodice up. Although she was trying to act composed, in reality, she felt anything but. She couldn't believe what she had just allowed... almost asked... to happen. She never made love casually, on a whim—even a demanding whim—and yet she just had.

This whole shanghaiing had gotten completely out of hand, she thought miserably, as the heat of her embarrassment over her incredibly wanton, unprecedentedly impulsive behavior flooded her cheeks.

She should have seen this coming. From the first moment she'd laid eyes on Nick she had known there was incredible chemistry between them. There were even times, like earlier today, when she felt herself liking Nick, empathizing with him, admiring his courage and determination under fire.

But to have made love with him, to have behaved so recklessly! For no other reason than that she wanted to be with him. This was a first—a first she intended never to repeat, Robyn schooled herself miserably. Reaching behind her, she tried to manage the zipper, but to her mounting dismay, her fingers were too clumsy to work it.

"Don't go," Nick said. He reached around gallantly to help with her zipper. His hands cupped her shoulders warmly. "Not like this," he whispered.

The touch of his hands made her tremble. Robyn realized she wanted him again as fiercely, maybe even more fiercely, than she had moments earlier. What was happening to her? Was it possible? she wondered, amazed. Could it be she was falling in love with Nick? Or was this simply some terrible yet predictable offshoot of her having kidnapped him? Did he desire her because they had both fallen prey to the Stockholm Syndrome? Or was, as she knew Leland would suggest, Nick only trying to use her, to seduce her into getting his way. Gaining his freedom.

Robyn shoved a hand through the mussed strands of her hair, pushing it away from her face. Leland had warned her that Nick would try to seduce her. And he had. What a fool she had been. What a silly, stupid, overly romantic, oversexed fool! She had known Nick was not to be trusted.

With a quick twist of her body, Robyn extricated herself from Nick's arms.

Nick read the distaste on her face and swore silently to himself. He knew it had been too soon. That he shouldn't have let it go so far. But he had, and now he would have to live with her anger. Or find a way to get around it and get her back into his bed.

"Robyn, please—" Nick said softly, knowing it wasn't like him to beg, but also knowing it had never been that good, that hot, or that sweet, with any woman. That kind of passion, chemistry, whatever you wanted to call it, was not something he was willing to give up. Nor, he thought grimly, should Robyn be so quick to thrust their tryst aside. Maybe their lovemaking had been foolhardy and sudden, but passion like theirs was also far too valuable to give up without a fight. But Robyn, it seemed, wasn't in the mood to listen to anything he had to say.

Just as he had feared she would, she sent him another arch look. She held up a palm to stave him off. "You can forget the sweet talk, Nick. I'm immune. I may have fallen into your sensual trap once. I won't do so again. Not today," she finished heavily. "Not ever."

Chapter Eight

"The door was unlocked," Robyn said in a stunned voice as she brought in Nick's dinner tray.

"Yes, I know," Nick said quietly. He hadn't left the room, hadn't even tried, because he had wanted to show her he could be trusted. That she didn't have to lock him in a room, or lock him out of her heart, to be safe from potential harm. His strategy appeared to be working. His captor looked severely shaken.

Robyn set the tray on the bedside table. She was wearing a long-sleeved teal silk shirt and matching trousers. Nick figured she had probably selected the outfit because, unlike the sexy, bodice-hugging, shoulder-baring dress she'd worn earlier, this outfit was loose and flowing and covered her from neck to ankle. And did absolutely nothing to dull her appeal. She was still sexy as hell. Disturbingly so.

"Why didn't you leave?"

Because of what happened between us earlier, Nick thought. He hadn't meant to make love to her like that, but now that he had, he couldn't just walk away.

He still cared about what happened to his mother, the business. Both were damned important to him. But not as important as Robyn, and what he had discovered between them.

Knowing, however, that she would reject such a notion out of hand, telling him it was too soon, Nick passed on the opportunity to tell her just how enamored he was of her, and said simply, with his usual amount of sass, "No car, remember?"

Robyn didn't so much as blink. "I'm serious, Nick," she said softly, her sable eyes still searching his face. "Why didn't you leave?" Especially when she had left the door open on purpose. She'd been half hoping he would make his escape so she wouldn't have to think anymore about what had happened between them earlier, or what very well might happen again, given half an opportunity. Like it or not, she was drawn to Nick. Hopelessly drawn to him in ways she couldn't begin to explain, never mind understand. She just knew that it was so.

Nick shrugged indolently but didn't move from his prone position on the bed. "I thought about it," he confessed.

Without warning, Robyn's heart was beating double, and then triple, time. She didn't want to make too much of this. But she couldn't ignore what he was saying, either. "And?"

"I just couldn't go," he said quietly. "Not without answers."

Five hours ago, Robyn would have denied Nick's request. But five hours ago they hadn't made love.

Five hours ago she had thought Nick's mother would call. But Cassandra hadn't yet called. And Robyn was beginning to believe, just as Nick already did, that Cassandra wasn't going to call. And that, in turn, could mean only one thing as far as Robyn was concerned—Cassandra didn't know about the kidnapping. Only Leland did.

If she'd done anything, even inadvertently, to hurt Cassandra...

Robyn sighed and sank into the nearest chair. She kept her eyes on Nick. Like it or not, maybe it was time they started trusting each other. Certainly it couldn't hurt to hear more of his side of things, especially since it looked as if Leland hadn't been straight with her. "What do you want to know?" she asked resignedly.

Nick surveyed the wary look on Robyn's face and decided to start with something easy. Right now she still didn't know who to trust, but hopefully, once she realized how fully she had been duped, that would change. He sat up and swung his legs over the side of the bed, bracing his hands on either side of him. "How did Joseito and Carlos get involved in this?"

Robyn exhaled a short, wavering breath and swallowed hard. "Basically, it was an exchange of favors. Leland promised to help Joseito get work papers in the States for his brother if he acted as driver and pilot."

"And you said he promised you a promotion?"

"Yes, my own line of clothes at Wyatt & Company."

"I hate to admit it, but having looked at your designs, I think that was a good move on his part and a smart business decision. What I don't understand," Nick said slowly, "is why any of you felt it was necessary to shanghai me to accomplish that."

"He can't give me my own line without expanding the company, and he was afraid your coming back and fighting him for control of the company would jeopardize the arrangements he'd made toward that goal."

"And you believed that?" Nick asked incredulously.

"After reading the threatening telegram you sent Leland, I did."

Nick's mouth set. "I sent Leland that telegram because I was furious with him for setting me up with those women."

Robyn gave him a patronizing look. "Come on, Nick. You're blaming him because you ended up in bed with four near-naked women?"

"And a photographer in the room, don't forget that. And hell, yes, I blame him," Nick ground out. "Had I not been slipped a Mickey, I never would've ended up in that situation."

Robyn bit her lip and studied him hesitantly. Nick could tell she wanted to believe him. "What does all that have to do with Wyatt & Company?" she asked.

"Isn't it clear?" Nick retorted, exasperated. "Leland wants me out of the picture."

"I thought you *wanted* to be out of the picture." Nick gave her a quizzical glance and she explained,

"Leland told me your mother offered you control of the company when your father died."

"That's true," Nick acknowledged, "she did."

"And you turned it down."

"Yes," Nick qualified, "but not for the selfish reasons you suspect me of. Wyatt & Company was always their baby, from the very first. My mother and father both nursed it along. When my father died last year, it was very hard on my mother. I could see her withdrawing into herself. She told me at the funeral she didn't think she could go back to the business ever again, that it was just too painful, and she wanted me to take over for her. She wasn't talking about beginning a new career or picking up a new interest, or concentrating only on her charity work, mind you, just withdrawing. I knew that would be the worst possible thing for her, so I said no, and rather than let her continue to lean on me to an unhealthy degree, I left. I figured she would pull herself together out of sheer necessity, like she always had. Instead, Leland stepped in and began to court her. He convinced her that what she really needed was not a good healthy devotion to her work, but someone to take over my father's role in the company again, someone to shoulder the responsibilities of CEO."

Nick's mouth twisted bitterly. "By the time I found out what was happening, it was too late. She had already married him."

"And that's when you stepped in and said you had changed your mind, you wanted to run the company again, because you didn't want Leland to have it,'' Robyn guessed slowly.

Nick shot her an aggrieved look. ''Where did you hear that?'' he demanded. ''No, let me guess. Leland?''

Robyn nodded, affirming his worst fear, that Leland was even slimier than he had suspected.

Nick sighed. He strode back to Robyn's side and took her hand in his. ''Listen to me, Robyn,'' he said earnestly, and looked deep into her eyes. ''That's not the way it happened at all.'' Robyn listened to him intently. ''After their marriage, Leland was pressuring my mother to step down from the business completely and let him run it alone, so she could devote herself entirely to leisure pastimes and the business of being his wife, but she was reluctant to do that because it had always been a family company. So she called me and offered one last time to let me assume the helm. When I realized she was serious about making Leland CEO now and possibly getting out of the business entirely in the near future, I knew Leland was up to no good.

''I told her I would come back, and booked a flight to Dallas the next morning. That was before the race. After the race, as you now know, I never made it back to the hotel in a conscious state. One minute I was in the limo. The next thing I have a memory of at all is awakening in bed with a hangover the size of Missouri and four scantily clad women. My mother was furious with me for the scandal, of course. At Leland's urging, she gave power of attorney to him instead, without discussing it with me any further, or even agreeing to hear my side of things.

"I found out about the power of attorney and I sent the wire to Leland to let him know the jig was up, that I was on to him. I knew he had been the one to set me up. Who else could it have been? He was the only one with something to gain." Nick exhaled his frustration roughly. "And I returned to Dallas only to have my mother put off our talk until after the symphony concert that evening. And the rest, as you know, is history. I was shanghaied to Mexico before I could even make her understand I was set up."

His words had the ring of truth. Robyn was sorry she hadn't listened to him tell his side of things sooner. And yet, she couldn't help but remember that Leland had warned her Nick would try anything, say anything to get her to come around to his side in the battle for control of Wyatt & Company.

"Your mother has always struck me as a very smart woman, Nick. If Leland is as bad as you think…why hasn't she realized this, too?"

Nick shrugged. "I don't know. Maybe because she doesn't really want to know. Maybe because she doesn't want to admit she made a mistake? Maybe he's just covered his tracks exceedingly well, at least with her."

Robyn paused. Everything Nick said made sense. His theory explained why she hadn't been able to talk to Cassandra thus far. On the other hand, like everyone else in America, she had seen the photos of Nick in bed with those women. He'd had a dopey look on his face, but he'd seemed to be enjoying their kisses and caresses nonetheless. She'd read the threatening telegram he'd sent Leland. And though Leland and Nick had a feud to settle, Leland had been nothing but kind and supportive to her. She couldn't forget that Cassandra Wyatt certainly seemed to trust him.

Despite all that, her gut feeling told her Nick was telling the truth. A very big part of her wanted to help him. But was that a rational move on her part, considering all that was at stake? Did she just want to help him because of the undeniable attraction she felt for him? Because she wanted to believe that their making love so recklessly had not been a terrible mistake?

Tightening his hold on her hand possessively, Nick continued earnestly, "Now, look, Robyn, I know Leland is up to no good. He has to be if he was willing to cajole you into kidnapping me to get me out of the way. The question is what else is going on right now? How is Leland planning to expand Wyatt & Company?"

Robyn drew a bolstering breath, deciding to go for broke and tell Nick everything. Maybe his reaction to Leland's activities would clue her in as to who was lying and who was not. "He's supposed to be meeting with outside investors all week to raise capital to expand Wyatt & Company and fund my clothing line," she said.

Nick blinked. "Outside investors!" he echoed, stunned.

"Yes," Robyn affirmed. Her knees were shaking. Deciding it might be a good idea to sit down, she moved toward the closest fixed object—which happened to be the bed. "He's trying to raise five million venture capital."

With a distracted, increasingly upset expression on his face, Nick sank down beside her. "Does my mother know about any of this?"

Robyn shrugged and tried not to think about the fact that Nick was sitting so close to her their thighs were touching. "I guess. I mean it's pretty hush-hush. Leland only told me because he wanted me to understand the necessity of getting you out of town as fast as possible no matter what. No one else in the company knows, I'm sure of that. Leland doesn't want news of the expansion getting out until the deal is set and officially announced."

"Have you ever talked about the expansion with my mother?"

"No, but then I never really see her, Nick, except in the departmental meetings that involve the new designs. Leland now handles everything on the business side."

Nick nodded grimly. Everything was swiftly falling into place. "Did you ever hear Leland discuss raising venture capital with my mother?" he asked brusquely.

Robyn thought back. "No," she said finally. "I never heard him say anything to Cassandra at all on the subject. But again, that's not uncommon, Nick. Your mother was never really involved in the business side of things, even when your father was alive. She was always much more concerned with the creative side—what types of fabric, and clothing, and styles we were working on. Those are the meetings she sits in on."

"I know." Nick sighed heavily and shoved a hand through his hair. "Unfortunately, that only made Leland's nefarious activities all the easier."

Robyn's heart was suddenly pounding. "What do you mean?"

Nick sent her a grim look. "My mother has roughly fifty million dollars. She'd never want outsiders holding stock in Wyatt & Company. It's a family business, not a public firm."

Fifty million, Robyn thought, staggered by the amount. To Nick, it seemed no more important than fifty pennies would have been. Rather, it was simply a fact of his life.

"Did she ever talk specifically with you about the new line bearing your name?" Nick asked.

Robyn shook her head negatively.

Nick's frown deepened. He reached over to absently take her hand. "Which means my mother doesn't know about Leland's plans," Nick continued worriedly, his dark green eyes intent as he squeezed her hand in his. "Because if she did, and she approved of Leland's plans to expand the company, she would simply give him the money to do so outright." He moved swiftly to his feet, pulling her with him as he moved. "I've got to warn her, Robyn."

"Okay," Robyn said, agreeing completely that this was something that needed to be cleared up with Cassandra Wyatt at once, for their mutual peace of mind. "We'll call—"

"No." Nick let go of Robyn's hand. Regarding her gravely, he said, "First of all, I don't want to tip off Leland that we're on to him. There's no telling what he would do. Second, my mother will never believe me without proof, not after all that's happened this week."

Robyn knew he had a point. She also knew that if everything Nick presumed about Leland proved to be correct, Leland had probably covered his tracks exceedingly well. Certainly he'd made a believer out of her. "How are we going to do this?"

Nick grinned, looking deliciously devil-may-care. "Ever play cops and robbers when you were kids? Well, this time it'll be like James Bond."

Nick was dashing enough to be a James Bond, Robyn admitted reluctantly, but it was more than just the sexy combination of his ash hair and dark green eyes, or the solid strength of him. It was the heart and soul of Nick that drew her, and would continue to draw her long after this unexpectedly unsavory episode in their lives was over.

Robyn tilted her face up to Nick's. "I want to help you get to the truth, Nick," she said. If Nick's suspicions were right, if she had unwittingly helped Leland swindle Cassandra Wyatt out of anything, she would never forgive herself. "Just tell me how I can help."

Nick's expression was filled with purpose. "Okay, here's where we'll start..."

"I PROMISE I'LL MAKE GOOD on my stepfather's promises to you all if you help me now," Nick finished speaking to Robyn, Carlos and Joseito.

"It's a deal," Robyn said, and the two brothers concurred.

"Carlos and I will stay behind at the villa," Joseito said.

"Right." Nick nodded. "It's important to keep up the pretense so Leland doesn't suspect anything is amiss."

Joseito frowned. "What will I say when he asks to talk to you, Robyn?" he asked.

Robyn hesitated. Leland wasn't a man to be put off, at least not for long. In that way, he and Nick were very much alike. "Tell him you'll have me call him back," she said.

"Yeah," Nick agreed. "Tell him she's busy with me." Nick turned to Robyn and sent her a glance that spoke volumes about his memories of their impetuous lovemaking. "Tell him," Nick said huskily as his eyes locked with Robyn's and he reached for her hand, "that I've fallen for her like a ton of bricks." His gaze roved her features lovingly before he continued softly and convincingly to Joseito. "Leland knows how beautiful Robyn is. He won't have any trouble believing that."

The problem was, Robyn thought, when Nick looks at me like that, I believe the fable, too. Could it be possible? Was Nick as interested in her as his ardent kisses and tender lovemaking attested? Or was he interested in her only because he needed to enlist her help to get out of this jam he was in, and felt—as Leland had predicted that he would—that seducing her would be the best way to insure her help? Worse, would his interest in her fade as soon as he got his company back?

But there was no more time for her to think about that, for Nick was already going on, taking command of the situation as skillfully as he had seemingly taken command of her heart. "Now, the first thing we have to do is share whatever knowledge we've picked up," Nick said, making contact with each member of the group Robyn had assembled. "Joseito, you've been driving for Leland for how many years?"

"One and a half."

"So you probably know more about him than any of us," Nick assumed.

"Probably," Joseito agreed.

Nick picked up a paper and pen, looking more the shrewd and skillful businessman than he knew, Robyn thought.

"Let's start from the beginning," Nick said. "And guys? Don't leave anything out."

"NICK, ARE YOU SURE we're doing the right thing?" Robyn asked as they parked in front of the Scarsdale, New York, mansion. Just over twenty-four hours had passed since they'd joined forces, and yet the change in Nick was nothing short of miraculous. Despite the obstacles facing him, he remained cheerful, resourceful. In short, he was a joy to be with, which made

Robyn's self-directed task of keeping a safe emotional distance from him all the harder.

The more she was with him, the more she grew to like him. And that could be dangerous indeed. When it was all over, Nick would no doubt want to put this stressful episode of his life behind him. That being the case, she didn't want to become more enamored of him than she already was. Making love with him once had been a mistake she could live with. Making love with him again, and then having him move on without her, would leave her with a broken heart.

Fortunately, their list of things to check out had left them with little time for anything but sleuthing and more sleuthing, Robyn thought as she followed Nick's gaze and looked at the half-dozen late-model luxury cars and limousines in the driveway. To her consternation, it was clear that a small, private party was going on inside the elegant home. "Maybe we should have called first."

Nick cut the ignition on their rental car. He flashed her a sexy grin, showing none of the nervousness she felt. "Never crashed a dinner party before, hmm?"

"Never even thought about it," Robyn admitted.

"Well, stick with me, babe," Nick said grimly as he pushed from the car and waited for her to circle around and join him in front of it, "and you'll do even more amazing things."

As they started up the walk, Robyn shivered in the cold night air. It was definitely winter in Scarsdale. Since it was January, she supposed they were lucky it wasn't snowing. "I just hope they don't make too much of a scene when they toss us out."

"Getting tossed out of here is the least of our problems at the moment."

Robyn paused and regarded him solemnly. She knew Nick was right to be worried about his mother. She was worried, too.

To Robyn's surprise, the door opened before they could ring the bell. A stuffy-looking butler greeted them at the door. He took one look at Nick and Robyn's clothes, which had been picked up at a department store at a mall they passed en route to Scarsdale and were casual at best, then sniffed and said, "Deliveries are made at the *back* door."

Nick held up a palm to keep the butler from shutting the door in their faces. "We're not here to make a delivery, pal," he said. "We're here to see Ms. Montgomery."

The butler drew back, as if he'd inadvertently been tricked into smelling some odious piece of trash. "Ms. Montgomery is *entertaining.*"

"Perhaps you'd be so kind as to tell Ms. Montgomery that Nick Wyatt, Mr. Leland Kincaid's stepson, is here to see her about a most urgent matter." Nick continued with a smooth confidence Robyn admired, "I think, in the interest of family privacy— mine and hers—that she will want to see me."

"One moment, please," the butler said stiffly. He shut the door in their faces.

"What if we get inside and she still won't talk to us?" Robyn asked.

Nick's lip curled sardonically. "Ms. Montgomery is Leland's ex-wife," he reminded her. "If anyone knows the dirt on him, she probably does." He shrugged. "Besides, if she feels even half the animosity I suspect she does about the sleazoid, I'm sure she'll be glad to share her feelings with us."

True, Robyn thought, as the door opened again. "Go around to the back door," the butler directed.

Nick and Robyn hurried around.

A beautiful woman in a long red velvet gown greeted them at the back door. She ushered them through the kitchen, down a long passageway and into a small sitting room. "Your timing is the worst," Ms. Montgomery said with a glare at Nick.

"I know," Nick apologized readily. "And I'm sorry. But we had to talk to you." Briefly he explained what Leland had done to him and his mother thus far. Leaning forward, his clasped hands between his spread knees, Nick continued in a highly confidential tone that could easily have charmed the wings off angels. "The thing is, Ms. Montgomery, that son of a bitch has driven such a wedge between my mother and me that I don't think she'll listen to me without proof."

"That's the way Leland operates," Ms. Montgomery said softly. She shook her head in silent remonstration, thinking not so much of Nick's situation, Robyn thought, but her own, whatever it had been.

"Divide and conquer," the woman continued. "First he alienates you from family and friends, making it look as if it's their fault, not his, of course.

And all the while he is romancing you like you've never dreamed."

I know a little about that, Robyn thought. Making reckless, foolhardy love with a dangerous man could be so enticing. Nick had shown her that. So well, in fact, that at the oddest moments, the most inappropriate moments, she found herself wishing he would show her again.

"Leland told my mother the two of you had just drifted apart," Nick said. "That the two of you had an amicable divorce."

"Oh, we stopped getting along, all right, but it wasn't any slow, gradual process," Ms. Montgomery said with more than a touch of bitterness. "More like a rude awakening on my part. A very rude awakening. I found out he had diverted ten million dollars of my money without my knowing it." She sighed heavily. "Rather than be publicly embarrassed about the way he'd conned me—his unethical actions were just the barest inch inside the law—I had my lawyers end the marriage with a small settlement and a minimum of fuss."

"Hence," Nick speculated, "his move to Texas."

Ms. Montgomery nodded. Her expression was grim. "I told him if I saw him making even the slightest move on anyone else, ever again, that I wouldn't hesitate to ruin him. He knew I meant it."

"Will you talk to my mother?" Nick asked.

Ms. Montgomery hesitated only a moment before she nodded. "Yes, Nick. I'll not only talk to your mother, I will bring legal action of my own against him. Leland Kincaid has got to be stopped before he does any more damage. I suppose I should have done something before, but I really hoped, naively I see now, that he had learned his lesson."

Having taken enough of Ms. Montgomery's time, Robyn and Nick said they would show themselves out. "She seemed like a nice woman," Robyn remarked after they had slipped back out the servants' entrance.

"Maybe too nice for her own good," Nick said, a troubled light in his dark green eyes.

"Do you think Leland's stealing your mother's money, too?" Robyn asked.

Nick shrugged and took her arm. He adjusted his steps to hers. "I don't know. Obviously, whatever Leland's up to has something to do with his attempts to raise venture capital. Who knows," Nick said, pulling Robyn in a little closer to his side, "maybe he wants to sell off and or close down parts of Wyatt & Company a bit at a time and this is part of his cover. I'll tell you one thing. I don't think the Young Junior division can be in near as much trouble as Leland has led everyone to believe, not when it has always been so financially solvent."

"So where now?" Robyn asked, pausing in front of the rental car.

Nick gave her another reckless smile. "The New York office of *Naughty Not Nice.*"

Chapter Nine

"Look, Wyatt, this is all very interesting, but seeing as how I don't know what the hell you are talking about," Darby Gibbs drawled, lounging back against the scarred wooden bar, "you and the lady here may as well be on your way again. I've got nothing to tell you."

Nick gave Darby Gibbs a feral grin and leaned in close. "Do you want to keep those teeth, Gibbs, or eat them for breakfast?"

It was a simple question, and backed with enough muscle to make Darby Gibbs pale to a nice light shade of green. Watching the two men, it was all Robyn could do not to grin. It hadn't been easy, tracking Darby down. First they'd had to go the *Naughty Not Nice* office in New York City. As it was after ten at night, none of the editors Darby Gibbs employed were there. The night watchman, however, had been only too eager to be bribed into giving out the address of Darby's favorite pub, a seedy dive that smelled of sour mash and cigar smoke, located a few blocks away.

Nick rested an elbow on the bar and leaned in a little closer. "You and I both know I was set up, Gibbs," Nick informed the tabloid publisher with exaggerated patience.

"All I'm asking is who arranged for me to grace the cover of your lovely tabloid with those four nubile ladies."

It was a simple enough request, Robyn thought, but one Darby was not fool enough, or drunk enough, to answer.

Darby braced his back against the edge of the bar and turned his gaze away from Nick's. He looked out at the other ill-groomed, rough-looking, hard-drinking patrons in the establishment. "Like I said, sport, I—"

Darby's words were cut off as Nick grabbed his shirtfront with both fists, hauled him off his barstool and to his feet. The action was swift and violent, and to Robyn's amazement, caused not even the slightest ripple of interest among the other customers. "You know," Nick said conversationally, "I could sue that rag you put out for so much money you'd never see your way out of the red."

Darby acknowledged that possibility with a faint shake of his head, then, lifting his glass around Nick's arm, he downed the last three swallows of whiskey in his glass in one long gulp. "You'd have to win first."

Nick raised his fist without any warning, hauling Darby up until the smaller man's feet left the floor and they were eye to eye. "After you left the hotel room, I went to a hospital emergency room. The doctors there took a sample of my blood and did some tests to determine what I'd been given. The colloquial term for it is a Mickey Finn—chloral hydrate and alcohol mixed together. So if I were you, *sport,* I'd think about the possible ramifications of being involved in a scam where an innocent person was drugged to the point of unconsciousness," Nick advised with lethal quiet as Darby Gibbs continued to dangle in front of him like a fish on a hook.

Darby's face flushed a bright red. His eye radiated fear. "Okay, okay," Darby sputtered, abruptly seeing the advisability of cooperating with Nick before he got his lights punched out. "Just let me go and I'll tell you what went down. Or at least as much as I know."

"I have a better idea," Nick said coolly, keeping a firm grip on Darby's shirt. He stared into Darby's bloodshot eyes. "You tell me everything you know and then I'll let you go."

Darby Gibbs gulped. Both of his hands came up to wrap around Nick's fist. "It wasn't my idea. The first I knew of your, uh, predicament with those dolls was when Harvey brought in the photographs."

"Harvey?"

"Yeah," Darby said, "he's one of our best. Always gets the celebrities."

Nick breathed in and out in the measured way of a man who was struggling to hold on to his patience and not having much luck at it. "Where is this Harvey now?" he ground out.

Looking into Nick's eyes, Darby began to tremble. "Out on a stakeout."

"Where?" Nick demanded.

"Central Park West." Darby let go of Nick's wrist long enough to fish in his pocket and come out with a small leather notebook. He flipped through it until he came to the page he was looking for, then held it up for Nick's perusal. Nick took it with his free hand, then ripped out the page.

"What's he doing there?"

"Waiting for a certain married movie star to come out. He's at a dinner party in the building."

Nick lowered Darby back to the floor, but kept his hand on Darby's shirt. "You're sure he's there?"

Darby bobbed his head up and down emphatically. "Harvey had a tip from the doorman. He's there, all right. And so are the four babes."

"The babes!" Nick repeated. "Why?"

"You might say Harvey is the kind of guy who likes to make his own opportunities—that is, if nothing else presents itself."

Nick stared at Darby, seething. "If you've lied to me, buddy, I'll be back," Nick vowed.

Darby didn't doubt it for a minute. Neither did Robyn.

"How much longer do you think we'll have to wait before Harvey and the women come out from wherever they've hidden themselves?" Robyn asked as she settled down beside Nick in the car they'd rented at the airport to help them get around New York.

"I don't know," Nick said, as he adjusted the focus on the videocamera. "Could be hours now or a matter of minutes. One thing's certain. If we see a movie star come out of that building, we'll see Harvey, and his entourage. And this time, I'm getting all the action on videotape so there will be no question later about exactly what happened here tonight.''

Robyn rubbed her hands together, warming against the chill of the car. It was a cold night, which looked to get colder still. Yet she didn't mind sitting there in the parked car with Nick; in fact, she was enjoying their derring-do. More, maybe, than she had a right to. ''I wonder if old Harvey is getting tired of waiting, too,'' she said.

''Probably not, considering that the women are with him. In fact, he's probably enjoying every minute of this.''

Robyn allowed herself a moment's jealousy—she hated thinking of Nick in bed with those four voluptuous women—then pushed it aside, realizing that particular night had been anything but pleasant for him. ''You really hate what Harvey and Darby did to you, don't you?''

Nick stretched his arm along the seat behind her. In the dim glow of the streetlight, he looked even more handsome. ''Believe it or not, Robyn, it's not my idea of a good time to wake up in bed with four half-naked strangers. Having my picture splashed on the front page of that rag was even worse.''

''You're humiliated by all this, aren't you?'' Robyn asked softly.

''It's not just that.'' Nick shrugged. ''Look at what it did to your opinion of me.''

Robyn turned to face him. "I admit I was a little fast to judge you," she confessed.

Nick grinned. "A little?" he queried.

Robyn blushed. "Okay, a lot."

Silence fell between them.

"Nick?" she said after a while, amazed that she could feel so content and so safe, just sitting next to him in the car.

"Hmm?" Nick asked, a distracted look in his dark green eyes.

"Have you ever been serious about anyone?"

He turned toward her once again. "No," he said, holding her eyes. His gaze softened. He reached up to briefly touch her cheek. "What about you?"

"No." And though Robyn had always lamented the lack of passion and romance and involvement in her life, suddenly she was glad there wasn't anyone. Except Nick.

"Why not?" Nick pressed. He leaned down to get his cup of take-out coffee from the cardboard holder on the floor. "I'd think there would be tons of guys beating down your door, wanting you to be their girl."

"There have been," Robyn confessed.

"Then—?"

"I always got bored."

Nick had, too. "How come?"

"I don't know." Robyn shook her head, not sure she could explain. All she knew for sure was that when she had kissed her other beaux good-night or spent time with them, there had always been something missing. Something vital. Except with Nick. When he had kissed her, she had felt complete. When she was with him, she felt an odd kind of contentment. And it didn't seem to matter that their alliance was just a temporary thing, born of sheer necessity and dwindling time. "Maybe the guys who want to date me aren't very exciting. All I know is that the romances I've had have always fallen far short of what I want in life."

Nick smiled at her gently. "Which is?"

"A passionate, wild, exciting, spontaneous kind of love." The kind she already had with Nick. Robyn arched a brow, adding, "Not the dull, excessively thought-out kind my sister has back in East Texas."

"Why'd she do that anyway?" Nick asked with a frown. If her sister looked anything like Robyn, it certainly couldn't have been for lack of male attention.

"I'm sure it was because of what happened when we were growing up," Robyn said. "My father was laid off from his job when we were both in junior high. Up until that time, our family had enjoyed a fairly affluent life-style, but suddenly, we were living on his unemployment benefits."

"It must've been tough," Nick sympathized as he reached down for another cup of coffee.

"More so on our parents than us," Robyn admitted as she took the cup he handed her. "Not that any of us ever felt the situation would be permanent," Robyn said, taking a deep draft of the steaming brew. "At least not at first." She sighed unhappily, recalling. "But as the months passed and my father failed to land another position with another firm, and his unemployment benefits ran out, it began to look very grim.'' So grim Robyn couldn't even begin to describe it to Nick.

She swallowed hard and forced herself to go on in the most matter-of-fact voice she could manage. ''So we moved back to Beaumont because we could live more cheaply there, and my mother took a job as a waitress in one of those twenty-four-hour coffee shops on the interstate. For the next few years, we lived on what she made, while my dad went back to school at Lamar University and took the courses necessary to get a degree as an accountant.'' Robyn paused and drew another deep, bolstering breath. ''It wasn't until we were nearly out of high school that everything went back to normal again.''

Nick let his arm drop from the back of the front seat to her shoulders. It curved around her like a soft protective cloak. ''It sounds like your parents really pulled together,'' he said admiringly.

''Yes,'' Robyn affirmed. She turned, so she was more snugly in the curve of his arm, and tipped her face up to his. ''They did.'' For a moment, she let herself just look into his eyes, into the compassion and understanding she saw in their deep green depths. ''But the experience left its mark on all of us,'' she continued softly. ''I don't think my father will ever feel as confident.'' Robyn paused to sigh her regret. ''My mother's become frugal to the point of ridiculousness.''

"And your sister married for security," Nick recalled.

"Yes." Both were silent a moment, then Nick flashed her a grin.

He chucked her under the chin, regarding her with a mock-serious glance. "And you have turned into a modern-day Robin Hood."

Robyn broke into a grin at his teasing tone. It was so nice, sitting here with Nick this way. So different than how it had been in the beginning, in the limo, and at the villa. "Why do you say that?" she asked.

"Because," Nick replied, "you'll do almost anything to prevent others from losing their jobs and suffering the trauma your family did. Including kidnapping me."

Robyn regretted the way they had first met, and why, but that was all. She wouldn't trade the past days with Nick for anything in the world. As difficult as they had been, they had also been the most exciting days of her life. The most passionate. And fulfilling.

"And yet you haven't married for security," Nick continued, amazed. "Instead, you embarked on a career that was filled with risks."

"I admit I've had my share of high and low moments there," Robyn admitted in a voice that reverberated with satisfaction.

"And yet you love every minute of it," Nick ventured.

"Yes," Robyn said with quiet emphasis. "I do." Funny, she thought, that she had never before in her life needed or wanted a man's approval. And yet here

she was, oddly pleased that Nick seemed not only un-
threatened by her strength, but extremely pleased with
it, as well.

"That's good," Nick said. "I can't imagine a life
more miserable than one where you hated what you
did to earn a living."

"I agree." Robyn sat up straighter as a flurry of
movement farther down the walk caught her eye.
"Omigosh, Nick, look. It's... it's Warren and Annette!"

Nick pulled his arm from her shoulders. "And look
who's coming out behind them—none other than my
old pal Harvey and his four bimbos," he said, his low
voice underscored with victory. He grabbed his camera and they both leapt from the car.

Nick turned on his video recorder and aimed it at
the group rushing Warren.

In a flash, Annette was shoved aside and Warren
was surrounded by the babes. Harvey clicked away
madly with his camera. Seeing how Warren was being
set up, the doorman leaped in to join the fray.

"We've got what we need! Let's get the hell out of
here!" Harvey called. He and the women turned and
headed toward a van parked halfway down the block.

Nick and Robyn circled around and raced to catch
up with them, Nick approaching the group from the
north, Robyn the south.

"Hey, Harve," Nick said casually as he popped the
film out of his video camera and stashed it in the inside pocket of his leather bomber jacket. He slammed
the cartridge door shut on his camera. "What's up?"

he asked curtly as he blocked their entrance through the van's side door.

Harvey paled visibly. Obviously, Robyn thought, he had recognized Nick. And why not? He'd probably made a tidy sum on that picture of Nick.

The women scattered, but Robyn had seen enough to know they were all the same women who had posed with Nick. She was further disgruntled to realize they were as beautiful and voluptuous in person as they were in the photographs.

Harvey paled even more when he noticed the video camera in Nick's hand.

"Nice scam you got going here, Harve," Nick began conversationally, though there was a decided edge to his tone. He patted the now-empty video camera in his hand. "It ought to make a nice piece on 'Entertainment Tonight.' Who knows?" Nick shrugged. "Maybe Warren and Annette might even want to use it as evidence in the lawsuit they'll probably bring against you and *Naughty Not Nice.*"

"I wasn't doing nothing wrong here," Harvey protested as he lifted both his hands in surrender.

"Sure you weren't," Nick agreed amiably. His dark green glance narrowed. "And goats fly." He paused, as calm as Harvey was panicky. "I want to know one thing from you Harve."

Harvey swallowed so hard his Adam's apple bobbed up and down. "And what might that be?"

"Who set me up?"

"I don't know what you're talking about."

Nick turned to Robyn with a smile that radiated purpose and energy. "Hold my camera, would you, sweetheart? It looks as if Harve here needs some persuasion."

Nick moved like lightning. One second he had the camera and there was a good two feet between him and Harvey. The next, Robyn had the camera and Harvey was flattened against the side of the van. Nick had a fistful of Harvey's shirt in each hand and his knee against Harvey's groin.

Harvey wheezed as he fought to regain the breath that had been knocked out of him when Nick slammed him against the van.

"I'm going to ask you one more time, Harve," Nick said, through his teeth, as his knee edged up another inch. "Who set me up?"

Sweat broke out on Harvey's brow. "Le—Leland Kincaid."

"How much did he pay you?"

"Obviously," Harvey grunted as Nick tightened his hold on his throat, "not enough."

Nick released him as abruptly as he had grabbed him. "That's all I wanted to know."

"That's all?" Harvey wheezed and clutched his throat with both hands.

"That's all," Nick said. He turned to Robyn. "Got the envelope?"

"Right here." Robyn handed it over. While Harvey watched in openmouthed astonishment, Nick slipped in the videotape, sealed the envelope and tossed it into the nearby mailbox. "Like I said, it ought to make a nice piece on 'Entertainment Tonight.'"

Harvey moaned and headed for the box. He jerked on the handle frantically, to no avail. So intent was he on his mission, he failed to see the policeman coming down the block.

"YOU THINK YOUR MOTHER will believe it?" Robyn said moments later, when they'd settled back into their rental car.

Nick sighed. "She'll have to, when she sees the same bimbos on television."

"What if they don't put it on the air?"

"With Warren and Annette?" Nick grinned. "They'll put it on. And if Warren has any sense, he'll really send a message to those folks and sue."

They both fell silent for a moment as Robyn thought how well Nick had handled his quest to unmask Leland. Not only had he avenged himself, but he'd effectively put a stop to such shenanigans by Harvey in the future. She turned to Nick. "Now what?"

He put the key in the ignition and started the engine. Nick glanced at his watch and saw it was after one, then backed from the parking space and headed out onto the street. "I suggest we head back to the Westchester County airport where we left the jet and try to find a room along the way. There are plenty of hotels out that way. We can head back to Dallas early in the morning."

"Okay," Robyn said. It had been a long day. More so for Nick than her, probably, since he had been the one to pilot the Wyatt & Company jet from Mexico to New York early that morning.

Unfortunately, it wasn't as easy to find a room as they had hoped. It seemed everywhere they stopped was already booked solid for the night. By the time they hit the fourth hotel, it was two-thirty in the morning and Robyn was exhausted.

"Got one room left," the clerk said. "And it's a king."

Robyn looked at Nick. Nick looked at Robyn.

"Up to you," he said. "If you want, I can sleep on the jet."

There was no heat in the jet, unless it was running. It was below freezing outside.

Robyn looked at the clerk. What choice did they have? Besides, it would only be for a few hours. "We'll take it."

"YOU'RE MAD AT ME, aren't you?" Nick said in a hushed voice as he unlocked the door to their room.

"No. Just tired."

"If you want, I can sleep in the car."

"You're being ridiculous, Nick."

"Am I?"

"Yes. We can handle this."

"You're sure?"

Robyn nodded stiffly. She took her suitcase from his hand and gestured toward the bathroom. "I'm going to get a quick shower."

"Fine."

She bided her time, hoping he'd be asleep when she came out. No such luck. He was lying on the bed, hands folded behind his head, watching a movie on cable.

His glance swept her jeans and shirt, but he made no comment about her attire. "My turn?"

Robyn nodded, wishing she didn't feel so awkward and ill at ease. So aware of everything about him.

Nick took a faster shower than she did, but his was also hotter, Robyn thought, judging by the steam that wafted from the bathroom when he stepped out.

He came out wearing jeans and a shirt, too, and sank down on his side of the king-size bed. Although Robyn had turned down the covers, neither of them had bothered to get under the sheets. He reached over, turned off the television and then the lamp beside him. The room was shrouded in semidarkness.

Nick lay back casually on his pillow, then turned toward her and propped his head up on one hand. "I'm going to need your help in Dallas, Robyn. I can't even get into the Wyatt & Company building anymore."

"Why?" Robyn asked, surprised. Though Nick looked relaxed and at ease, she was stiff with tension. As exhausted as she was, she was never going to be able to get to sleep, not with him lying next to her this way.

Nick frowned as he answered her question. "Leland had my badge deactivated."

Until now, Robyn had been under the impression
that Nick needed her along, to help him vindicate his
name. But as she reflected on the day they'd had together, she realized that she had actually done very
little, except to tag along and keep Nick company. He
hadn't needed her at all, except to break into Wyatt &
Company tomorrow. Abruptly she wondered if that
was the real reason, the only reason he'd asked her to
come with him, so he could have use of her badge and
knowledge of top-secret company codes. As she realized that might very well be the case, Robyn's spirits
plummeted fast.

"Look," Nick said, "if this is going to bother you,
our sharing a bed..."

It wasn't the sharing the bed that was getting to her
so much, Robyn reflected, as the absence of any real
chance at more lovemaking. Lovemaking that had
been reckless and foolhardy in the first place.

"It's fine," Robyn said stiffly. She rolled away from
him. She wasn't sure what it was—fatigue, or Nick's
business-only attitude—but she was suddenly very
close to tears.

Nick's voice came at her, soft and gruff. "Is it the
way I roughed up Harvey that's bothering you?" he
asked. Touching her shoulder, he rolled her onto her
back, so he could see her face. "Look, I know I was
tough back there, but after what the jerk did to me,
the guy had it coming. Those photos really hurt and
embarrassed my mother."

The last thing Robyn needed in her frazzled, exhausted, stressed-out state was more reminders of

Nick in bed with those four women. She turned away from his beseeching gaze and rolled away from him once again. "You don't have to explain, Nick."

"Then what is it?" Nick demanded after another moment's tense silence. Robyn continued to offer him her back and said nothing. "Is it those women we saw tonight? Is that what's got you so ticked off?" Nick persisted. "Seeing them in person? They meant nothing to me, Robyn. Nothing."

She rolled over to face him, furious with herself for caring what he felt or didn't feel for her—except convenience. And she was furious with him for noticing her unhappiness. "Thanks for sharing that with me, Nick," she said sarcastically, temper flaring. "I am so glad to know that those women—and probably dozens others—" *including me!* "—meant absolutely nothing to you."

He stared at her, mouth agape. "What's with you tonight?"

"I don't know, Nick. Maybe it's your attitude. Maybe it's everything you say and do?" Or *don't* say and do! "Tell me something, Nick," Robyn said, knowing she was behaving and sounding more irrational by the moment but unable to stop herself. She sat up, dragging the blankets with her. "What in this world, besides your standing with your mother, does mean something to you?"

"This," Nick said. Before Robyn could do so much as draw a single stunned breath, he had pushed her flat, swung his body over hers and wrapped his arms around her. His weight crushing her down onto the bed, he lowered his mouth to hers. Her lips parted, seemingly of their own volition, and his tongue swept into the deepest recesses of her mouth, bringing with it a firestorm of sensation and feeling.

And in that instant Robyn knew what the problem was. The problem was that she loved Nick, loved him with all her heart and soul. And she knew, deep down, from everything that had gone before in his life, that he would never love her back, not the way she wanted him to.

Furiously she tore her mouth from his and pushed him away. How could she have done this again? How could she let herself be seduced by a man who didn't even believe in the concept of romantic love, never mind actually feel it for her.

Nick released a shuddering breath. "I take it that's a no?"

Robyn shoved at his chest until he rolled off her. "You're damn right that's a no!" she said.

"Why?" Nick asked curtly. Why had she turned him down? He had felt her response. Dammit, she wanted him as much as he wanted her. It was good between them, they had already proven that.

"Because when we make love again," Robyn rasped breathlessly before clarifying slowly, and with great effort, "if we ever make love, I want it to mean something, Nick!"

Nick stared at Robyn. Dammit, if she wasn't the most impossible woman he had ever met! "What do you think, that I do this with every woman that comes down the pike?"

Robyn arched a brow. "Don't you?"

Nick fell silent. He had no answer for that, at least none that she would buy. Just as he had no explanation for the sudden rush of possessiveness he'd been feeling whenever he looked at Robyn today.

The truth of the matter was, their lovemaking did mean something to him. In fact, much more than he had expected it to, in ways that went far beyond the superior physical satiation she had given him, far beyond the emotional support, understanding and simple backup she had offered him on this long, hard day. Nick laid back and folded his hands behind his head once more as he struggled to understand Robyn's hurt and indecision, and his own feelings. What did she expect of him? A pass and a declaration of love? Or simply that he stay on his side of the bed. And why did it suddenly matter so intensely to him what she felt?

He hardly knew her, and yet she was all he thought about.

He hardly knew her, and somehow she had become the top priority in his life, so much so that he had stayed in Mexico hours after he could have easily made another escape attempt.

Did this mean he was falling in love with her? he wondered, stunned, then realized with slowly dawning clarity that the answer to that was yes. But how could that be, he wondered, when he had known her such a short time? God knows, he didn't want to fall into the same trap his mother had. He didn't want to make a mistake by jumping into a relationship during

a stressful time of his life, just because it offered him
more emotional comfort and peace of mind than anything he'd ever done in his life. He didn't want to be
ruled by passion rather than rational thought.

Chapter Ten

Robyn woke slightly after seven to find Nick kneeling beside the bed. He had a ribbon-wrapped newspaper in one hand, a disposable cup in the other. "What is this?" she asked sleepily as Nick put the cup down on the bedside table next to her. Pushing the tangle of dark, silky hair from her eyes, Robyn struggled to sit up.

One hand on her shoulder to keep her from leaning back, Nick slid a pillow between Robyn and the hotel bed headboard, then placed the newspaper on her lap. He picked up the cup, removed the cover and folded her fingers around it. "This, is what we call a peace offering."

Robyn inhaled the scent of amaretto-spiced coffee. "*USA Today* and a cup of coffee?"

"Two of the things you missed the most while we were in Mexico, if my memory serves me correctly."

Robyn wondered what time he had gotten up, and how far he'd had to go to find the amaretto coffee. "You didn't have to do this, Nick," she said quietly,

trying but failing not to be touched by his efforts to
please her. She met his assessing, apologetic gaze
bravely, then recalled with dismaying clarity the reason he felt he had to patch things up. They'd come
close to making love again last night. They would
have, if she hadn't come to her senses.

"You didn't have to go to all this trouble," she said
as she thought about the way he had kissed her, and
how much she had wanted to give in to him, even
though she knew she couldn't. "I would still have
helped you get into Wyatt & Company corporate offices, pass or no pass."

Nick's face slashed in a rugged grin that let her
know he felt no ambivalence about the desire he felt
for her, only frustration that they hadn't made love
again last night. Did he think a few well thought-out
gifts from the heart would accomplish what his kisses
hadn't, a bending of her will?

Nick studied her face and swore softly. "I knew you
would take this the wrong way," he said, as if her wary
reaction to his gifts were just what he had expected. He
got down on one knee beside the bed and rested both
wrists on his propped-up thigh. In the leather bomber
jacket, white oxford-cloth shirt and jeans, he looked
both handsome and faintly dangerous. "Let's get
something straight right off the bat. I'm apologizing,
Robyn, not attempting to buy you."

His reading of her feelings was astute and on target. Robyn felt the ice she had erected around her
heart melt just a tad. Could it be . . . was she softening
toward him already? When she'd only been awake a

few minutes? If so, it was not because of the inherent sexiness of his dark green eyes or the wind-tossed layers of his ash blond hair, or the clean, wintry scent of his hair and skin. It was because...oh, hell, he was doing it to her again! One whiff of the chemistry between them and she was behaving like a romantic fool.

"Oh, Nick," she said softly, nodding to the gifts he had brought her, "no matter what we call all this, doesn't it all amount to the same thing?" He wanted in her bed again, whereas she only wanted to keep her heart from breaking.

"No," Nick said firmly, his gaze never wavering. "It's not the same thing at all, Robyn. I'd never buy a woman." He pressed his index finger gently against her lips to stave off her interruption. "I admit," he said gently, his eyes telling her it was so, "I shouldn't have tried to make love to you last night. I shouldn't have kissed you like that."

Oh, yes, Robyn thought, melting just a little, even after he had taken the warmth of his fingertip from the softness of her lips. Yes, you should have, Nick. Because I wanted you, too. "But you did," she reminded him.

"Yes, I did kiss you," Nick said firmly in a way that let her know he had absolutely no conflicting feelings about his passion for her, "and you kissed me back. Like you meant it."

I did mean it, Robyn thought, with all my heart. And that was precisely the problem. She knew she was romantic to her toes. She wasn't sure Nick had even one truly unabashedly romantic thought in him. Oh, she knew he was as sensitive a man as he was strong, and caring. He didn't want to hurt anyone. His bringing her the peace offering was proof of that. He knew he'd hurt her, and he wanted to make it up to her. Somehow. She just wasn't sure he could. Not without telling her he was in love with her and proposing marriage, and she knew that wasn't about to happen!

"Maybe we should just be friends, Nick," she suggested quietly.

He gave a nod. "Do you think that's realistic? Considering the chemistry between us?"

"I think it has to be." Robyn folded her arms across her breasts. "Besides, our time is running down. We have to get back to Dallas."

Nick had no quarrel with that. He got lithely to his feet. "Which brings up something else," he said. "Just to be on the safe side, I don't think we should fly in to Alliance, DFW, or Love Field. My mother's friends are all indefatigable travelers and are always flying somewhere, and so are the sales reps for Wyatt & Company. There's too much of a chance we'd run into someone we know and they'd mention it to either Leland or my mother in passing."

"You're right," Robyn agreed. "There's no use taking any chances that Leland could be tipped off about our being back in Dallas before we have a chance to gather all the proof against him we need." She finished downing the coffee he had brought her, then put the cup aside. She tossed back the covers and swung her feet over the bed. "So where should we fly in?" she asked, knowing from the look on Nick's face he had already formulated a plan. "Houston? Oklahoma City?"

"I've got an even better idea," Nick said with a smile. "I've got a friend, Travis Wescott, who has a private airstrip outside of San Angelo. We could land at his ranch, borrow one of his ranch pickups, and drive on in. There's much less chance of us running into anyone we know and rousing Leland's suspicions that way."

It would take longer that way, Robyn knew. But they had time to kill anyway, as they wouldn't want to risk showing up at Wyatt & Company until everyone else was long gone for the day. "You're sure you can trust this Travis?"

"With my life."

"Okay then, let's do it." That decision made, Robyn crossed to the dresser and picked up her hairbrush. She dragged it through her hair, restoring order as best she could. Finished, Robyn put down the hairbrush and turned back to Nick. "Speaking of Leland, don't you think it's time I gave him another call?"

Holding her eyes, Nick nodded. "But first, let's call Joseito, just to make sure everything's still okay on their end, too."

To ROBYN'S RELIEF, Carlos and Joseito were fine. Which left her with the disagreeable task of calling and checking in with a man she no longer trusted. "Leland? Hi." Robyn worked to make her voice as normal as possible. "It's Robyn."

"Robyn!" Leland chastised her immediately. "Where the hell have you been? I called you last night!"

"Yes, I know," Robyn said, having already learned as much from Joseito, "but I thought I should wait until this morning, when you were at the office."

Leland paused. "Good thinking. I don't want Cassandra upset any more than she has been by Nick."

But this wasn't Nick's fault, Robyn thought, it was theirs. In retrospect, she wondered how she had ever fallen for Leland's lies. Was it because she had just thought the worst about Nick because of who and what he was?

"So what were you doing last night when I called that you couldn't come to the phone?" Leland pressed in a tone that was both fatherly and concerned.

Robyn pressed her temples as static crackled over the line. "Didn't Joseito tell you I was with Nick?" she asked, recalling the possessive way Nick had kissed her.

"Yes." Leland paused. "He also said the two of you were really starting to get along."

Robyn blushed at the innuendo in Leland's tone. Out of her peripheral vision she could see Nick lounging in the door to the bathroom, listening to every word she was saying. "Ah, yes," she stammered slightly, aware despite her efforts not to that she was starting to blush, "we were…are…getting along. Pretty well, as a matter of fact."

"Robyn, Nick hasn't…he hasn't seduced you into losing sight of our goals, has he?" Leland pressed.

"No, of course not," Robyn lied, though in truth that was exactly what Nick had done. Seduced her into switching sides, changing allegiances. Clutching the receiver tightly, she selected her next words as carefully as she would have picked her way through a mine field. "I'm just trying to see that he enjoys himself while he is down here, Leland." She inhaled a deep, ragged breath.

Nick grinned and made a face that left no doubt in Robyn's mind what he was thinking about.

Blushing even more, she rushed on before Leland could ask her anything else. "I don't mind telling you Nick was a handful when we first arrived. I wasn't sure we were going to be able to handle him at all, until—"

"Until what?" Leland prodded with interest when she didn't go on immediately.

Until we made love and everything changed, Robyn thought.

"Until he accidentally saw me sunbathing in a bikini," she lied, knowing she couldn't tell Leland the real reason everything changed. "Then . . . well, everything seemed to get a lot better. Nick no longer seems to resent being in Mexico. In fact, he's almost mellow about the whole thing."

"Well, that doesn't surprise me in the least," Leland said. "Nick always was a womanizer. Cassandra said the number of girlfriends he's had numbers in the hundreds."

Great, Robyn thought.

"Unfortunately, none of them last long. So, do your best to drag things out, just for a few more days, Robyn."

Robyn glanced up to find Nick pointing to his watch.

"I don't know, Leland. I've been able to hold Nick off so far with the promise of what might be, but I don't know how much longer that's going to work. He's starting to get impatient."

"Just another twenty-four hours, Robyn, that's all I ask. By 9:00 a.m. tomorrow, everything will be in order. You'll be able to let Nick go and come back to the States."

Nine tomorrow! Robyn thought. That didn't leave them much time. "What happens if Nick tries to press charges against us?" she asked.

"He won't, if for no other reason than to spare his mother a second public scandal. I promise you, Robyn," Leland finished firmly, "everything is going to be fine."

NICK WATCHED Robyn as she hung up the phone. He sat down on a corner of the unmade bed. Even though time was running out, he wasn't particularly anxious to leave the haven they had made. "You okay?" he asked, aware now, as he had been earlier, that Robyn didn't like lying.

Robyn clasped her hands together. "Sure."

Nick continued to study her face. "Talking to him upset you," he guessed.

Robyn lifted her head to his. "It made me feel like such a fool."

"Because there was a time not too long ago when you believed he was a nice guy?"

"Partly," Robyn admitted as she gazed into Nick's dark green eyes. He hadn't shaved yet this morning, and the day's growth of beard gave him a dark, piratical look she found ruggedly appealing.

"And the other part?"

"Because I'm starting to get too caught up in the moment. We never should've kissed each other again last night, Nick."

"I disagree. I think that's exactly what we should have done. And if we had more time, I'd do it again."

At his declaration, Robyn's heartbeat doubled. "I want us to be friends," she insisted.

It was ironic, Nick thought, how many times he had delivered that same speech to lovers in the past. Now, at the time in his life when he least wanted to hear the same from a woman, she was hitting him with it right between the eyes.

"I want more than that," he said firmly, and it had taken only one night sleeping beside her, platonically sharing a hotel room bed, to convince him of that. Like it or not, he was not going to be able to just walk away from Robyn at the end of this, and never look back.

She would always be on his mind. He would always remember the way she had melted against him when they'd made love, the way she fervently returned his kisses, the way she seemed able to take from him even as she gave and gave.

They couldn't just let chemistry like this go. Which opened up the door to a long-distance relationship. Nick had never tried one, mainly because his interests kept him moving around so much, but maybe it was time he did.

He knew if he could make a setup like that work with anyone, it would be Robyn. In fact, he looked forward to the interludes between some of his races, when he could come home to Dallas, and to her. He could see it now. Robyn would cook for him. Hell, maybe he'd even cook for her. They'd talk and catch up on each other's lives, then end up in bed the rest of the night, insatiably making love. Now that, he thought, would be the life.

Unfortunately, Robyn looked so anxious at just his declaration of desire he feared she was about to faint. Maybe this wasn't the time to bring up commitments and complications. But soon, he promised himself firmly.

"I won't push you," Nick continued seriously. He smiled as the pinched look on her face began to fade and her slender shoulders relaxed. He gazed deep into her eyes. "I'll wait until you're ready for more."

"I WONDER WHAT your mother thinks you've been up to all this time," Robyn said as she settled into the cockpit next to him and strapped herself in.

Nick frowned as he adjusted the jet's altimeter. His mother's wrath was the last thing he wanted to think about at the moment. "It's hard to know."

"If she doesn't know you were kidnapped. Or went to Mexico—"

"I'm sure she doesn't."

"Then she must be very worried about you, since you missed your meeting with her."

Nick began the process of backing the jet out of its parking space and onto the runway. "What's this?" he asked, his eyes on the airport employee guiding him. "You suddenly think I'm reliable now?" Nick grinned, recalling her initial reaction to him. "Whatever happened to the selfish, self-pitying, unreliable playboy heir?"

Robyn blushed. "Now that I've gotten to know you, I see you have a serious side. Your mother must know that, too."

"She did," Nick confessed gravely. "But that," he continued, fighting the bitterness that threatened to wrap around his heart, "was before my father's death."

"What happened to change that?" Robyn asked quietly, studying his face with more compassion and understanding, Nick thought, than any man had a right to even hope to find in the woman he wanted to spend the rest of his life coming home to.

Nick guided the nose of the jet to the end of the runway, then waited for the signal that it was their turn to take off. He could see four other jets in front of him, so he knew it would be a couple of minutes. "In a word, Leland."

Robyn watched as Nick inched them forward, one place at a time. "Did your mother know you disapproved of Leland before she married him?"

"Yes, but she thought the animosity between Leland and me would pass, once we got to know each other better. The next thing I knew she and Leland had eloped."

"How did you take the news?"

"Badly. I thought it was too soon. Dad had just been gone six months." Nick's voice caught. "Anyway," he forced himself to go on, "I wasn't in a good frame of mind when I met up with Leland again, and the minute my mother's back was turned, he let me know that he was running the show now, and that if I knew what was good for me, I'd go back to my race-car driving and my women and leave my mother and him alone." Nick sighed, recalling the ugly conversation. "In retrospect now, I see that he probably figured I'd go right to my mother with a report on him— which I did. My comments only infuriated my mother. She'd only seen Leland behave charmingly toward me. So the rift, already widening, was made even bigger at that point. Like a fool, I played right into Leland's hands." Nick shook his head regretfully.

"Oh, Nick," Robyn said. She reached over to take his hand.

Nick covered her small hand with his and squeezed it tightly, taking comfort in the warmth and understanding she offered. "Anyway," he went on, "after that, I stayed away. My mother and I rarely spoke, and when we did it was usually because of some family occasion or holiday. Our relationship was definitely strained."

"And yet," Robyn said in a soothing voice, "when it came right down to it, she offered you the company again."

"Yes." Nick nodded, remembering how he had felt when that phone call came. Burdened, because the job was clearly out of his realm of interest, at least in the fashion sense. And elated, that she trusted him with something that meant so much to both her and his late father. The potential problems aside, Nick had known from the start there was only one path to take.

"And I was willing to take her up on the offer," Nick continued easily, looking into Robyn's sable brown eyes, "if only to try and find some way to mend the distance between us."

They were silent as Nick got word from the control tower that they were next. For the next few minutes, he concentrated solely on the mechanics of takeoff. Only when they had reached their assigned altitude and were cruising comfortably did Robyn speak again.

"If we are able to expose Leland, if your mother rescinds the power of attorney she gave Leland and kicks him out, will you still return to Dallas and run Wyatt & Company?"

She looked torn about the prospect of that, Nick noticed, as if part of her would welcome him there, whereas the businesswoman assumed that he would be more in the way than a help. "I don't know," he answered her honestly. "So much has changed. I guess it would all depend on what my mother wants when the dust from all this settles. If she needs me, certainly I'll be there."

Robyn thought about Cassandra Wyatt. She had always struck Robyn as a very strong woman, although she had been taken in by Leland, just as Robyn had. Like Nick, she could see the outcome of the brouhaha they were about to create going either way. Naturally, she wanted Nick to have a reason to stay in Dallas on a permanent basis. And she wanted him where she could see him, often. But she was equally aware that after she and Nick exposed his mother's husband for a sleazy, no-good fortune hunter, Cassandra might not want either of them around as a reminder.

At the thought of Nick leaving Dallas again, maybe for good this time, Robyn's stomach clenched. The muscles in her neck grew tense. Still, she had to ask, for her own peace of mind. If there was no reason for her to be fantasizing about happy endings, she needed to know it now. "And if your mother doesn't still want you to stay on and be part of the company?" Robyn asked.

"If she doesn't, I'd prefer to be driving," he said honestly. To Robyn's disappointment, he looked entirely unambivalent about that decision. "But before we can talk about that, Robyn," he said, "we need more proof."

"THERE'S NO NEED to whisper, Nick," Robyn said as they walked into the tall office building in downtown Dallas hours later. "It's two in the morning. The staff of Wyatt & Company is dedicated, but it's highly unlikely anyone else is working at this hour."

"I guess you're right."

She slipped her badge into the electronic reader next to the elevator going up. Seeing a security man, Robyn lifted her hand in a wave. She was glad she had insisted they stop by her apartment so she could get her briefcase and portfolio and change out of her casual clothes and into a business suit. The more normal she looked, the better, she had theorized, and seeing the warm reception from the guard, she knew she had been right.

"Hey there, Ms. Rafferty. What brings you out so late?" the guard asked.

"Would you believe work?" Robyn shook her head, then pointed her thumb to Nick. "He got so excited about my designs for the new resort line when we were talking about them over dinner that he insisted I show them all to him tonight."

The security man smiled at Robyn. "Well, don't stay here too late, Ms. Rafferty. It's not good for you to work so hard."

"She's here a lot after hours?" Nick prodded.

The security man nodded. "That is one employee who's married to her job!"

"Married to it, eh?" Nick said, as the two of them stepped into the elevator.

Robyn punched the button for her floor. "Like you're not devoted to yours."

He lounged against the wall of the elevator and pointed a thumb at his chest. "I'm not at it all day and night."

Robyn grinned at him. Neither was she, normally. "But you do keep a schedule that not only makes you travel constantly but prevents you from having a serious relationship with any woman," she said.

Nick shrugged. "So I like the travel, the publicity and the parties that go along with my job." Without warning, he backed her into a corner of the elevator, an ardent look in his eyes. "It isn't the hours I keep or the career I chose that has kept me single, Robyn."

Robyn looked up at him and knew he wanted to kiss her. Knew she wanted it, too. "Then what is it?" she asked breathlessly.

Nick cupped a hand under her chin. "Until now, I just haven't met the right woman. But maybe that will change." He leaned closer, his thumb tracing the line of her cheekbone. Their lips were about to touch when the elevator doors slid open.

Nick straightened. Once again, he was all business. "Come on." He took her hand in his. "We've got a job to do."

Getting into Leland's office was easy, since Nick still had the key that had been given to him by his father. Getting into Leland's most up-to-date files was not. "The damn computer's got a lock on it," Nick hissed.

"Maybe we don't need that," Robyn said.

She picked up the appointment book on Leland's desk and opened it to the following day. His calendar was full, starting with a breakfast meeting at seven-thirty, in the executive dining room. "I recognize some of these names," Robyn said, frowning unhappily as she quickly put two and two together. "They're corporate raiders, Nick."

A chill went down Robyn's spine as understanding dawned. "Nick, you don't think...Leland wouldn't be trying to sell the company out from underneath your family, would he?" she asked, aghast at the nefarious possibility. She stared at Nick, racked with guilt. The fact that Leland was meeting with the corporate raiders proved beyond a shadow of a doubt that he had not been trying to expand Wyatt & Company, but sell it off and disassemble it, piece by piece. For profit.

If she had only listened to Nick earlier, Robyn chided herself miserably, and let him explain, then this wouldn't be happening now. Wyatt & Company wouldn't be in jeopardy. Nick would not still be estranged from his mother. She thought of all the employees whose jobs were now in jeopardy, and felt even more ill. If anyone became unemployed over this, she would never forgive herself.

Nick's face became dark and brooding as he contemplated Leland's appointment book. "I wouldn't put anything past my sleazy stepfather," he said between his teeth. Taking her hand, he propelled her

swiftly out of the high-backed swivel chair, aware, as
was she, that they had wasted far too much time as it
was. "Come on, let's go. My mother has got to be
warned."

Chapter Eleven

Cassandra heard the muted nighttime ring of the princess phone beside her. She picked it up before it had finished its first soft ring. Beside her, Leland continued sleeping soundly. "Hello," she whispered into the phone.

"Mom, this is Nick, but please don't say a word," her son said in a rush, giving her no chance to vent her considerable anger at him. "Just listen to me. I need to talk to you right away. I'm downstairs in a car parked at the front gate. I'd come in if I could but I can't. Mom? Please? Come out and talk to me."

Your timing stinks, Nick Wyatt, Cassandra thought wearily. *And considering the way you've hurt, embarrassed and disgraced me, I really don't owe you a thing.* Except...he was still her son, and current disasters aside, she still loved him more than life. "All right," Cassandra whispered, and gently set down the phone. *But your explanation for disappearing on me like that had better be a good one, Nicholas Wyatt.*

Leland stirred briefly. He yawned and opened his eyes as Cassandra reached for her slippers, then he glanced at the clock. "What's going on?" he asked sleepily.

Cassandra smiled at her husband reassuringly. There had been enough trouble between Nick and him already. They didn't need any more, and certainly not tonight, when it seemed Nick was finally coming to his senses about her remarriage, at long last! "It's nothing, darling. I can't sleep. I'm going downstairs." Which was the truth, she thought, as far as it went.

To her relief, Leland nodded and closed his eyes.

Grabbing the satin robe to her peignoir set, Cassandra stole out of the bedroom and padded down the stairs. Wary of walking down the driveway in her nightclothes, she stopped at the front hall closet and retrieved her trench coat. At the end of the driveway was a passenger van. Nick stepped out to help her inside. To Cassandra's relief, Nick looked fine, which made it all the more inexcusable that he hadn't even called to let her know he was all right.

"I ought to wring your neck, Nicholas Wyatt," Cassandra began, then stopped as she realized that she and her son weren't alone.

"Robyn?" Cassandra said, stunned to see one of her most valued young designers there, too.

Robyn smiled back at her tremulously. "Hello, Mrs. Wyatt."

What did Robyn have to be so nervous about? Cassandra wondered, and why was she here with Nick anyway... holding his hand like that? Oh, no, Cassandra thought, with a fast-sinking heart as she noticed the undeniable tension and closeness between Robyn and Nick, a new, almost startling, intimacy between the two young people that even a child could have picked up on. Surely the two hadn't eloped!

"Mom." Nick let go of Robyn's hand and held up both his palms in a gesture of surrender. "I can see you're jumping to all sorts of conclusions here."

"You noticed?" Cassandra said dryly.

"And we'll get to everything, I promise," Nick continued, "but for right now, Robyn and I have an awful lot to tell you, so I want you just to listen."

Cassandra accepted the cup of steaming coffee Robyn handed her. She loved her son dearly, but sometimes his constant need for adventure was a real pain.

"All right, I'll listen, but first, is there some reason the two of you couldn't come into the house so we could have this discussion like civilized people?" she asked.

Nick's expression turned grim. "A very good reason," he affirmed, and then began to explain. Cassandra was silent, listening. It was a lot to absorb, and yet, once she thought through the confused tangle of anger and embarrassment, it all made sense. Lately, so many things had not added up. Now, at last, she finally knew why.

"So you're telling me," she said slowly, long moments later, still feeling a little stunned as she looked at Nick, "that Leland was not only responsible for drugging you and planting those pictures of you in the tabloid, but that he talked Robyn into kidnapping you, as soon as you did return to Dallas?''

Robyn nodded, for a moment looking fearful that Cassandra would hold this against her. "He said it was imperative for the expansion to go through," Robyn explained bluntly, then paused and took a good look at her boss's face. "But you didn't know about that, either, did you?''

"No, I did not!" Cassandra snapped, irritated to find she had been so long in the dark, but determined to take full charge of the situation now. "Apparently, my husband has been a very busy man. What a clever liar he is. I should've known all along he was too good to be true. And now here he is, trying to sell Wyatt & Company out from under me, too," Cassandra summed up heavily at last.

Nick nodded grimly, looking as if he wished he hadn't had to be the one to break this news to his mother. "It appears that way, yeah. Sorry, Mom. Sorry I didn't come back sooner. That I got mad at you for marrying him in the first place, even if he was a snake. I know now that was really your decision to make. And I'm sorry for all the time we were estranged." For a moment Nick choked up, as did Cassandra, and Robyn, too. "I don't want that ever to happen again," Nick said at last.

"Me, either." Cassandra hugged her son tightly, glad the crisis had brought them together. "Oh, Nick." Cassandra released a long, sad sigh. "We've both behaved foolishly since your father died. And we've both suffered for it," she said, a little mistily.

"But we're okay now," Nick comforted his mother.

"Yes, we are, aren't we?" Cassandra wiped her eyes. As she looked over at her son and his companion, she couldn't believe all that he and Robyn had weathered, and yet they appeared to have come through it in top form. In fact, better than top form. The two of them had obviously fallen in love with each other, even though they hadn't said as much. Yet. She suspected they soon would.

Cassandra accepted some more coffee from the thermos. "I'm sorry, too, Nick," she said softly, after a moment, "for what Leland put you through." She shook her head in amazement. "I can't believe he actually had you kidnapped! Or that he talked Robyn into doing it!"

"We're all guilty of being manipulated by Leland," Nick acknowledged frankly.

"You're right," Robyn said with a sigh, casting another fond look at Nick. "We all played right into his hands."

"But no more," Nick said, with a serious look at his mother. "If that CEO position at Wyatt & Company is still open, I'd like to take it."

"What about your racing?" Cassandra asked.

"I'll find a way to do both," Nick promised. "The important thing is, I just don't ever want to let you down again, Mom. I don't want to let the company down. I owe Dad—and you—that much."

"Of course you can have the job," Cassandra said hoarsely. She leaned forward to hug Nick again. And this time she held him tight for a long moment.

Robyn ducked her head, tears flowing from her eyes. Maybe she'd been part of what had kept Nick and his mom apart, but she was also part of what had gotten them back together again.

Finally the two drew apart. All three of them wiped their eyes. "So, now that's settled," Cassandra said.

"It's time to get back to business," Nick concurred. "And unfortunately for us, we don't have much time. Leland's meeting with those corporate raiders is set to take place at seven-thirty. It's five now, and Leland still has power of attorney."

Cassandra toasted Nick and Robyn with her cup, then finished her coffee in a single draft. She gave Nick a steely look, letting him know with that one glance that the woman he had loved, respected and admired all those years was no longer grieving her husband, but back in full fighting force. "Let's go, kids," Cassandra said firmly. "It's payback time for dear old Leland. And this time, I'm in charge!"

"WHERE IS SHE?" Nick fumed, as he paced in front of the Wyatt & Company building. "It's seven twenty-five! My mother promised to be here half an hour ago."

Robyn walked anxiously at his side. She was every bit as worried as he was. "Obviously, there was some glitch in getting the legal papers drawn up and ready for her to sign."

"What if she got caught in traffic?" Nick's grim expression grew even grimmer. "What if—?"

Robyn held up a silencing hand. "Don't worry, Nick. You're mother's fine and she'll be here any minute. Unfortunately," Robyn said, glancing at the employees already beginning to stream into the lobby, "we can't risk waiting for her any longer. We're going to have to go with our contingency plan."

Nick looked her in her eyes. "You're ready to storm the executive offices with me?"

Although she knew her actions could very well mean the loss of her job, Robyn smiled and kept her eyes locked with his. She'd never felt such a rush of feeling for anyone as she did at that moment. And it wasn't just chemistry any longer. She felt, because of all she and Nick had been through together, that they had somehow joined souls and spirits, too. "I think I owe you this one," she said softly.

Nick grinned at her roguishly, desire emanating in his dark green eyes. He took her hand tightly in his. "Get your badge out and let's go."

They entered the building and stepped into the elevator. Robyn and Nick were the only occupants left on the elevator by the time it reached the executive floor. They headed directly for the executive dining room.

Leland's secretary stood as they passed her desk. "Wait a minute," she said. "You can't just go back there!"

"The hell I can't!" Nick called over his shoulder. "My family owns this company!"

Robyn was fast on his heels as Nick shouldered his way into the dining room.

As they had expected, Leland and four men in suits sat at the dining table. Seeing them, Leland's glance was quick and angry. "This is a private meeting," he said tightly. "Please leave."

"And what happens if I don't?" Nick challenged, folding his arms across his chest and bracing his legs. He regarded Leland contentiously, just daring him to try something now, in front of all these witnesses. "Gonna have me kidnapped again... *Dad?*"

Leland's mouth tightened momentarily, then he turned to his distinguished guests with a hearty smile. "This is my stepson, Nick. No doubt you've all heard about his escapades. The latest of which landed him and four half-naked women on the front page of a supermarket tabloid."

A murmur of disapproval rumbled through the dining room.

"Amazing what money can buy, isn't it?" Robyn asked. She turned to the men and pointed an accusing finger. "Leland was behind that, too."

Leland stared at both of them in a threatening manner, then said heavily, "Nick, Ms. Rafferty, as I've told you, I am in the middle of a meeting here."

"Oh, I know. You're trying to sell the company out from under us," Nick said.

"Your mother gave me power of attorney because she didn't want to be kept apprised of what was going on here. In fact, she has had no real, abiding interest in Wyatt & Company since your father died, Nick. That is why I'm selling the company to these gentlemen."

"What about my line, Leland?" Robyn asked.

"You'll have to take that up with the new owners," Leland said stiffly.

Robyn stepped closer, not above making a hysterical scene. Anything to delay the proceedings until Nick's mother showed up. "Wait a minute," she cried plaintively, like a woman scorned. "Leland," she wailed, "you promised me—"

"I said you were quite talented, Ms. Rafferty," Leland corrected. He turned to his guests and gave them a bear-with-me-fellas look. "I said it was quite possible you would one day have your own line with the company, but that is all I said!"

Robyn had been angry before. Now she was furious. "He's lying!" Robyn said.

"And he does it quite well, doesn't he?" Nick agreed.

Leland's glance narrowed. "Gentlemen, I think the sooner we conclude the business part of the meeting, the better."

Nick stormed forward, ready to start a physical brawl if need be. "You can't do this, Leland."

Leland picked up the telephone beside him and punched in a number. "Call security. Get them up here immediately." He hung up the phone. "You have two minutes, Nick. Maybe less. Unless you want to go to the police station, I suggest you vacate the premises immediately."

"And I suggest," Cassandra Wyatt said breathlessly as she strode in to join them, still in her nightgown and overcoat with her attorney close on her heels, "that you gentlemen be aware of this. I have just rescinded your power of attorney, Leland, and filed for divorce. You no longer have any authority in this company. Nor are you welcome in my home."

"Cassandra—" Leland looked stunned. And hurt. But Cassandra wasn't buying it.

"Cut the bull, Leland. I know who and what you are now. While I was waiting for the papers to be typed up, I had a long and very interesting conversation with your ex-wife. She in turn told me about your other three wives. Wives I knew nothing about."

Nick had to hand it to his mother. She'd taken the ball and run with it. "You're in a heap of trouble, buddy," Nick said to Leland.

"Thanks to my son, and this wonderful young woman," Cassandra said, stepping forward graciously and linking arms with both Nick and Robyn, "you are no longer in my life."

Security rushed in. "Have Mr. Kincaid escorted from the building," Cassandra said. "His guests, too."

Her orders were quickly carried out.

Robyn, Nick and Cassandra faced one another. Relieved the crisis was over, with the only real damage to their pride, Nick embraced his mother. "I was worried about you."

"I'm sorry, darling. But drawing up a new set of papers and having them witnessed and notorized was no easy task. Then we got caught in traffic trying to get over here. But I wasn't worried. I knew I could count on the two of you to hold up the proceedings until we arrived. And you did.'' She smiled at both Robyn and Nick.

"Will it really be that easy to get rid of Leland?'' Robyn asked.

Cassandra's attorney smiled. "He can either cooperate or go to jail for kidnapping and fraud. Besides, I don't think he wants anyone looking too closely into his past.''

Nick studied Robyn. "You look beat.''

"Two days with very little sleep will do that to a person.''

He wrapped an arm about her waist. "I'm taking you home,'' he announced.

Robyn was too tired to argue. The two of them said goodbye and headed out. Neither spoke much until Nick pulled the rented van up in front of her apartment.

Robyn knew she should make it easy on both of them and just get out of the car, but something in her couldn't let go that easily. She turned to Nick and sighed. "Well, I wish I could say it had been fun...'' she drawled.

He laughed and stepped out of the van. Walking around to help her with her door, he said, "Some parts of it were very fun.''

True, Robyn thought, very true.

They fell into step as they headed inside and took the stairs to the second floor. Suddenly, it was beginning to feel like a date. A very long, very intense date. One she wanted never to end. Feeling more reluctant than ever to let him go, she unlocked her door, then leaned against it with a sigh. Damn, but he looked good, she thought, even after all they had been through in the past twenty-four hours. It was going to be hard saying goodbye to him.

The pragmatist in her also knew it wasn't going to get any easier. And so once again, she lifted her eyes to the dark green depths of his. "It really is over, isn't it?" she asked softly, the romantic whimsical part of her wishing their relationship didn't have to end. Not yet.

Nick nodded and confirmed with a satisfied smile, "The derring-do part is, yeah. Not the business part." He braced one arm against the wall beside her head. "How do you feel about the vice presidency of Wyatt & Company?"

He said it so casually, and yet, it didn't sound like a joke. Robyn stared at him. "You're kidding, right?"

Nick shook his head. "Now that I'm back in the company, I have the power to offer it to you. And I'm dead serious."

Robyn swallowed, aware her heart had begun to beat very fast, and that it had less to do with the job he had just offered than the closeness with which he was standing to her. "I don't know what to say," she managed hoarsely at last.

"That's easy." Nick's green eyes sparkled, but he made no move to get any closer. "Say yes."

As if it were that simple, Robyn thought. "Oh, Nick."

Nick's eyes lost some of their zest. "You're turning me down?"

How could she explain? "It's my own line I want," Robyn said.

"You'll have your own line, plus the vice presidency," Nick said enthusiastically.

"Oh, Nick." Beside herself with happiness, Robyn looped her arms about Nick's neck. But what should have been a simple kiss of gratitude soon turned into much more. Their bodies pressed together through the clothes. Their mouths were so in sync, it was as if they were one.

"Oh, God," she whispered against his mouth when they paused to take a breath. How was she ever going to live without him?

His chest lifted and fell with the intensity of each deep breath. He kept his eyes on hers. "Let me come in."

There was no hesitation on her part. No rational thought. She just knew she had to have him, be with him, this one last time. They might have to say goodbye soon, but she wasn't ready to do that yet. Not until they'd been together once more. Robyn lifted his hand to her mouth, pressed a kiss against his palm and led him inside.

He had been there before, earlier in the evening. He'd sat in the living room while she changed clothes.

He hadn't seen the bedroom. No larger than the hotel room they had shared the night before, it was infinitely cozier, infinitely her.

Nick sank onto a brass bed with flowered sheets. The room smelled of her perfume, fresh and flowery.

Her discarded clothes were everywhere. He smiled at the untidiness.

Robyn kicked off the pumps she'd worn and unlooped the single strand of pearls from around her neck. "I'm not very good at this," she whispered.

"The hell you're not," Nick said. Recalling the way he had taken her in Mexico, swiftly, aggressively, up against the wall, Nick was determined to do it differently this time. Determined to make every moment last. The fierce ache was still inside him, demanding release. But his heart was in charge now, not simply his passion for this sable-haired, sable-eyed beauty.

Nick took her hand and tugged her down beside him. "Trust me," he whispered against her mouth, as he took her in his arms once again, "to do it right this time."

"Oh, Nick," Robyn whispered back, snaking her arms about his neck and pulling him down onto the mattress beside her. "Don't you know you've never done it any way but right?"

Nick rolled so she was beneath him. "Keep talking, babe," he said, grinning. "You're doing wonderful things for my ego."

She grinned back, teasing. "As if your ego needed any inflating."

Nick kissed her again, gently this time, then with slow-building passion. For every second they'd hurried before, he made it last tenfold. For every time he had hurt her with his words or deeds, he tried to make it up to her, tried to let her know with touch how much he cared. And he received it back in every seeking whisper of her tongue against his, every caress of her hands on his back. In the way she molded her body to his.

Afraid his weight might be too much for her, he rolled onto his side and then over onto his back. Robyn came with him. She landed on his chest, sable eyes alight with devilment. "You know what, Nick Wyatt?" she whispered impatiently as she opened the buttons on his shirt and tugged the hem from his jeans. "You're wearing too damn many clothes!"

Nick grinned and obligingly helped her get him out of his jacket and shirt. "I'm not the only one," he said, as Robyn reached for his belt buckle, and dispensed with that and undid his zipper.

"So do something about it," she whispered with a sultry grin.

Nick did. Seconds later, both were as naked as the day they were born. He knew it embarrassed her, but he couldn't keep his eyes off Robyn. She was just so damn beautiful. It was as if she had been made for him, all five feet nine inches of her. Her breasts were perfect round globes, her tummy flat, her hips round, her legs sleek. Just looking at her, he felt himself grow hard as granite.

He leaned down to taste one taut nipple, then the other. Robyn shivered. It wasn't enough. He had to have all of her, taste all of her. "Lie back, sweetheart, and let me love you," Nick whispered.

Robyn did as he asked. "Oh, Nick," she whispered as she shut her eyes, her lashes falling like thick dark arcs against her golden cheeks.

To Nick's growing pleasure, there seemed no end to her responsiveness. Robyn trembled and moaned as he made a leisurely tour of her body, and the more she felt, the more it ignited his own desire. He wanted to do everything with her. When her climax came, it was almost enough to send him over the edge, but Nick held back, waiting until she had stopped shaking before he slid his body over hers and started all over again. Kissing. Touching.

She was on fire by the time he slid into her warm, wet heat. Her skin was hot to the touch, her body ripe, her mouth rapacious. And still it wasn't enough for him, not when he knew this might be the last time, the only time.... He dove into her, measuring his strokes, keeping them slow and deep until at last she cried out and surged against him restlessly. Sensation rippled through him with the intensity of lightning.

"Now, Nick," she whispered as she wrapped her arms about his back and her legs around his waist. "Now..." she whispered, lifting her mouth to his, kissing him deeply. Until they were communicating at a level beyond words. Locking hearts, souls and wishes. And Nick was diving over the edge, falling into pleasure and finding a peace unlike any he had ever known.

Chapter Twelve

"Nick?" Cassandra's melodious voice floated over the telephone lines. "I thought I might find you there."

"What's up?" Nick asked as he switched the phone to his other ear.

"Your sponsor called to remind you that you have a race tomorrow."

Nick bit down an an oath. He had forgotten all about that. Which wasn't surprising, considering he had just spent the most satisfying night of his entire life, in Robyn's apartment, in her bed. Even now, when he'd lost count of how many times and how many ways they had made love, he still couldn't get over the wonder of having her in his life.

Not that his sponsors would be interested in that.

"I'll give them a call. Thanks, Mom."

Robyn was watching him intently as he hung up. She slipped from the bed and began to dress. As she put on a robe and slippers, Nick explained what his mother had said.

"Where's the race?" Robyn said when he had finished.

Nick studied her face. He could see no discernible change in her expression, but he could feel her slipping away from him. It was almost as if, to her anyway, the night of wild, abandoned lovemaking hadn't happened.

Keeping his eyes on her face, he answered, "Daytona."

Robyn nodded, taking that in. She walked into the bathroom and splashed cold water on her face. "When do you leave?"

Nick pulled on his jeans and followed her as far as the doorjamb. Her hair was a tumble of sable waves, her lips pink and bare and slightly swollen. There was a hint of color in her cheeks. Awareness of him? Nick wondered.

Knowing she was waiting for him to tell her when he was leaving, Nick turned his mind from their lovemaking and back to the time of his impending departure. The corners of his mouth turning down unhappily, he said, "I'll have to go soon."

Robyn's face fell. She said and did nothing, merely stood there, looking to all the world as though she'd lost her best friend.

"I'm sorry." Nick stepped forward and took the damp washcloth she held cradled in her hands. He tossed it aside and wrapped his arms around her, pulling her close. "I was hoping...I would've liked to have had a week or two in the sun." He drew back far enough to see her face. She didn't look any happier. In fact, her expression hadn't changed at all. "Maybe you could come with me," he suggested hopefully.

Here it was, the moment of truth, what she had been dreading all along. The time for them to get back to their normal lives. Lives that were spent far from each other.

"Is that a yes or a no?" he teased, cupping her chin in his hand.

Robyn closed her eyes and pressed a tiny kiss into his palm. She savored the time they had left, as much as she savored the wonderful night they had shared. "I wish I could say yes," she admitted softly.

"But you can't," he guessed, his tone neutral.

She shrugged and brushed past him, heading for the kitchen. She'd make coffee. Being immersed in normal activity would help. She wasn't going to cry.

"I've already been away from the office a week," she told Nick over her shoulder, amazed that her voice could sound so steady when her whole world was falling apart. And just when she finally had everything she had ever wanted. "I've really got to go back." *Just as you have to go back.*

"I understand." Nick nodded calmly. "You have enormous responsibilities at Wyatt & Company, just like I do now." Nick was going to be busier than ever if he tried to keep up with Wyatt & Company business and still race.

Robyn spooned amaretto coffee into the filter. "Maybe I could see you race some other time."

"Sure." Nick walked away from her, as casually he would walk away from any stranger he met on the street. He leaned against the counter, his hands shoved into the front pockets of his jeans. "I understand. Listen," he said, running a hand through his hair. "If

I don't want my sponsors any madder at me than they probably already are, I better get dressed and get going.''

Robyn nodded. ''Right.''

He went back into the bedroom. Robyn finished putting the coffee on, and then, unable to bear being away from him any longer and knowing their time together was almost at an end, she went back into her bedroom to watch him dress. To her consternation, he was almost through.

It was her turn to lounge against the jamb. She slipped her hands into the pockets of her robe. ''When's your next break?'' she asked calmly.

''I race every weekend for the next three weeks, then I get a weekend off.''

He wasn't going to have time for her. ''I see.'' This was going to be much harder than she thought. In fact, she wasn't sure she could do it.

''Robyn . . .''

Nick held out a beseeching hand, but Robyn turned away from it and led the way back out into the living room, her strides quick and measured. She knew she was going to fall to pieces the minute he left, but she would be damned if she did it in front of him. Life just wasn't fair sometimes, but that was the way it was. Nick had responsibilities to the company and his mother now. Plus, he still wanted to continue to race. He was going to be burning the candle at both ends. There was no place for romance in a schedule that jam-packed, and certainly not the kind of time-consuming commitments of love and marriage that she yearned for.

She ran a shaky hand through her hair, then spun on her heel so they were face-to-face once again. "I have a feeling this is the place where we're supposed to make promises to each other, Nick."

"But you don't want to," he guessed, his expression impassive.

Keeping the pain she was feeling tightly in check, Robyn shrugged. Watching him leave, knowing it would be weeks before she saw him alone again . . . if she ever saw him alone again, was about as much as she could take at this point. "Realistically, I don't think we should." Especially when she knew full well that once his memory of the kidnapping dimmed, he might not *want* to see her again. At least not in any tied-down sort of way. And she wasn't interested in being anyone's occasional pit stop. Not even Nick's.

He was quiet a long moment. "You're running away from me, Robyn. I can feel it." Color flooded her face as he drew a deep breath, took a step nearer and rested his hands on her shoulders. "Is it because of the way we got together?"

"Were thrown together," she corrected, acutely aware of the warmth radiating where he touched her. "And you have to admit they weren't the most normal of circumstances."

"No, they weren't." Nick looked down at her and grinned that sexy playboy grin of his. "But the feelings we have for one another are *very* normal, Robyn."

And bound to go unrequited in the long run, Robyn thought wryly. Mutual lust wasn't enough to build a relationship on, any more than mutual compatibility was. She didn't want to be like her sister, and find out she'd made a mistake, that Nick didn't love her the way he should after all.

She withdrew herself from his hands and paced some distance away. She could smell the coffee brewing, but knew when it was finished that she probably wouldn't want any, and neither would Nick. Not the way things were going. "Look, Nick," she began with difficulty, as soon as she had collected her thoughts, "right now you're grateful to me—"

"Grateful," he echoed, stunned.

"Because I helped get you out of a bad situation," Robyn continued, aware there were times—like now— when Nick made her feel like some spinsterish schoolmarm lecturing a postadolescent male student.

Nick closed the distance between them. "Only after you first helped get me into it," he pointed out sagely.

Robyn frowned at him. "You know what I mean," she reprimanded sternly.

"Yeah, I do, and you're wrong, Robyn," Nick said, taking her in her arms. "What I feel for you isn't gratitude," he insisted.

Robyn pushed away from him. She didn't want him holding her like that, so tenderly and so close, when he was getting ready to leave for three incredibly long weeks. "Then maybe it's the Stockholm Syndrome," she said.

"It isn't that, either." Nick dismissed the idea with a frown.

"Then what is it?" Robyn asked as she agitatedly paced back and forth.

Nick's brows quirked upward like twin thunder-clouds. He planted both his hands on his hips. "Does it have to have a name?" he demanded.

Yes, Nick, she thought. It does. It has to be love or it will never ever work between us long-term.

But Nick didn't tell her he loved her. Judging by the grim expression on his face as he regarded her, it didn't even occur to him. "You're making this impossible," he said.

She was being impossible! He was the one who could make love to her all night long, as if she were the only woman on earth for him, but wouldn't allow himself to love her—in a romantic, emotional, non-sexual sense!

"I'm trying to be realistic," Robyn bit out. And an affair with a man who didn't even believe in romance, never mind actually have time for it, just wouldn't work with her.

"Realistic or aloof?" Nick quipped, looking more unhappy and disapproving of her than ever.

Robyn clamped her hands against her waist, hating the defensive way he made her feel. "I admit I don't want to be hurt," she confessed calmly, telling herself she could handle this, that she could handle him!

Nick shook his head. "What makes you think I'll hurt you?"

"I didn't say you'd mean to," Robyn countered, exasperated, rounding on him. "But realistically, Nick—"

"There's that word again!" He warned like a bull about to charge.

"My life is here," Robyn continued matter-of-factly, ignoring his aggravated look. "And yours is...well, it's more than full, isn't it?"

"Thank you, Sherlock," he said dryly.

Robyn ignored his stab at humor. These were serious issues they were discussing. "Have you forgotten that conversation we had about why you'd never worked at Wyatt & Company before? Because you couldn't bear the idea of working a nine-to-five job and living in one place..." Which was exactly what she wanted and needed most out of life. The security of knowing she had a place to go home to every night, a place to go to work every day. She'd have enough of the day-to-day existence when her father was unemployed.

"That was before I fell for you," he insisted. "Before I changed my mind and agreed to work for my mother during the week and race primarily on the weekends."

Fell for me, Robyn thought, latching onto the words he chose to describe his feelings for her. Not fell in love with, but fell for me. Like a teenager with a momentary crush, a crush that would fade because Nick had made it perfectly clear he didn't believe in romantic love, period. Or hasty marriages or love at first sight. Lust was dependable in his book, even healthy, but not love. Never love. And, Robyn admitted miserably to herself, she couldn't live without love.

Determined not to let him see how much he could hurt her in the future, in fact already had hurt her, she said, as pragmatically as possible, "Look, Nick, let's face it. Our courtship, if that's even what it was, was filled with excitement. But now we're back to the real world. I don't want promises made that neither you nor I will be able to keep. I'd rather we just say so long now, and then—'' she grappled with the words, swallowing hard ''—take it day by day and see what happens.''

Nick stared at her as if she were a stranger. "And suppose I can't live with that?" he asked in a low voice that vibrated with vehemence. "Suppose I want a commitment from you today?" he asked hotly.

"What kind of commitment?" she volleyed back. "A commitment as a mistress?"

"What's wrong with being my lover?" he thundered back, reminding, "It suited you fine last night!"

"Last night was last night."

"Well, what about today?"

What about today? Robyn wondered. What about tomorrow?

Was she going to end up like her sister?

Her sister had married on a whim, because it had seemed like a good idea at the time. Because she wanted that kind of security with a man and was afraid it wouldn't be there if she waited before saying yes. And now ten years, countless luxuries, and two children later, she was miserable. Utterly miserable. Robyn shook her head. She was not like her sister. She wouldn't jump into a long-term situation without first taking plenty of time to think things through. She wouldn't be pushed into a corner. She had embarked on this affair with Nick on a whim, but it wasn't anything that was carved in stone. Maybe their affair couldn't be undone, she reasoned hotly. But it didn't have to be furthered. At least not now, with reckless promises made when he was walking out the door.

Robyn offered him her back and stared out at the sunny January morning. It looked so peaceful outside. In her apartment, everything was mixed-up.

"I can't talk about this anymore, Nick," Robyn said, heading for the door.

"Why not?" Nick asked as he blocked her move to show him out.

"Because I don't want to be rushed into anything I'm not ready for." And she was definitely not ready for becoming a rich playboy's hometown mistress.

"Funny," he reminded her sardonically, "you didn't seem to have a problem letting me rush you into bed."

Robyn's face flamed and she offered him her back. "That was different!"

"Why?" Nick clamped his hands on her shoulders and spun her around to face him. "Because there was immediate pleasure in it for you?"

Robyn wiggled out of his grasp and away from the front door. "You're being crude," she accused.

And you, he thought, are being cruel. Not wanting her to see how much she had hurt him with her abrupt dismissal, he merely shrugged and said, "So sue me. I like to know where I stand." His gaze raked her up and down. "I guess now I know, don't I?" Not waiting for her to reply, he brushed past her.

Her robe wrapped around her tightly, Robyn followed him to the front door. "Nick, where are you going?"

He turned with his hand on the knob and delivered his parting shot. "Where I belong! Back to the race-track."

"THAT'S SOME TROPHY you've got there," Joseito said admiringly several weeks later, as he came back to the pit where Nick and his crew were loading his car onto the truck.

"Yeah, it was a big one, all right," Nick said, appreciating the fact the two brothers had come to see him race, even if it was at the urging of his mother, who now employed them both. Cassandra was worried about him and worried about Robyn. She made that clear every time she phoned Nick or saw him at the office.

His mother was right to be worried, Nick thought. He wasn't happy. He hadn't been since he and Robyn had called it quits.

The business was okay. His mother and Robyn had a firm hold on the creative side. He had no problems with the business side of things. He'd studied business in college, had gone on to earn an M.B.A., and learned the ropes under the tutelage of his father during all those summers in between.

The problem was, his life just wasn't the same. Racing seemed more stressful than fun these days, even when he won. It was as if all the adventure had gone out of it for him now, or maybe it had gone out a long time ago—about the time he started winning regularly on the circuit—and he just hadn't really noticed, or let himself think about it, because he had no place to go. But now he was thinking about it all the time, wondering how to get the challenge and adventure back.

And then, there was his personal life, or lack of it. He hadn't had a date with another woman since he and Robyn had broken up, and he didn't want one. Every day without Robyn by his side, loving him and helping him and challenging him to be more giving and more noble than he thought he ever could be, seemed a little duller and emptier, and he feared those feelings were only going to get worse as time passed.

"Watching you race . . . fantastic!" Carlos agreed.

Nick smiled at Joseito's little brother. "Thanks. How's life at my mother's back in Dallas?" Funny, he had never thought much about home before when he was on the road, but now, whenever he was away, Dallas was all he could think about. Maybe because there he at least had glimpses of Robyn in meetings, and snatches of business-related conversation with her.

"Your mother, she is an excellent employer for both of us," Joseito said.

Nick smiled, glad everything on that score had worked out all right. Cassandra had pulled a lot of strings to get Carlos's work papers so quickly. "Carlos finally got his green card then?" Nick asked.

"Yes." Joseito smiled with relief. "And with your mother's help, he is going to apply for citizenship, too."

Nick was glad about that. Somehow, he felt his mother would be better off having the two brothers there on the premises to watch over her and size up any other potential beau. Not that he figured his mother would ever be sucked in by a fortune hunter again. They had all learned their lesson about that.

Finished overseeing the movement of his race car, Nick thrust his hands into the pockets of his coverall and sauntered away from the pit. "Everything okay with Robyn, too?" Nick asked.

Joseito nodded, his face lighting up at the mention of Robyn's name. "You miss her, *sí?*"

Nick shrugged. "I got used to her sticking to me like glue, you know. But it's okay."

Joseito said nothing. But then, Nick thought, he didn't have to. His skeptical look said it all.

"Look, what choice did I have but to get on with my life and she with hers?" Nick asked irritably. Especially after the way she had kicked him out without so much as even considering his request that they try to make a relationship between them work. "She certainly had no trouble getting on with hers."

Even if he couldn't stop remembering the way she kissed or looked in bed, her sable hair tumbling about her slender shoulders, her dark eyes alight with desire, closing with pleasure. The image haunted him daily, and more often than not, made his heart constrict with the kind of pain Nick had never imagined an unromantic guy like himself could feel.

Carlos stepped between Nick and Joseito. "I don't know about that," Carlos said. "I don't think Robyn is feeling as fine as she wants you to think, Señor Nick."

Joseito gave his younger brother a sharp look commanding him to silence. His heart racing at the idea of Robyn in any kind of danger, or sticky situation, Nick probed for more information. "What do you mean?" he asked anxiously. "She's all right, isn't she?"

Joseito and Carlos exchanged a look. "Of course she is all right, Nick. She even went to the symphony the other night."

Nick frowned. He'd like to think of the Meyerson Symphony Hall as their place. The two of them had met there, after all. "Who was her date?" He knew he sounded like a jealous fool, but he couldn't help it. He had to know. "Anyone I know?"

Carlos and Joseito shrugged, said nothing.

Nick felt himself become even more tense. "Dammit, is there something . . . someone . . . I should know about?"

"You're saying you care for Robyn?" Joseito asked cagily.

"Care? Hell, yes, I care!" Nick stormed. He had never once said he didn't!

"But not love," Joseito ascertained, looking for a moment like an overprotective father scrutinizing his teenage daughter's date.

"Love!" Nick echoed uncomfortably. "What the hell is love, anyway? Oh, I know about the feelings you have for family. The kind that are generated by long-term relationships—of course you come to care for them, and about them. But this thing between a man and a woman . . ." Nick paused.

Carlos grinned with all the optimism of a twenty-three-year-old. "It is good, *sí?*" he asked, elbowing Nick in the side.

Yes, Nick thought sourly, that was precisely the problem. It had been damn good! So good he couldn't forget it. Nonetheless, he wasn't fool enough to let a few days of passion alter his life, not in any permanent or irrevocable way. "I don't believe in love at first sight," he said flatly.

"Then you are not just one of the luckiest, wealthiest young men I know, but also a fool," Joseito said with a disapproving shake of his head. He continued to regard Nick with scorn. "Because sometimes, Nick, my friend, that is exactly the way it happens."

"YOU STILL MISS HIM, don't you?" Cassandra Wyatt said softly at eight the following evening.

Robyn looked up from the fabric swatch she'd been studying, pretending to be more distracted by her work than she was. She and Cassandra were the last two people still at work that evening.

"Who?" she asked blankly.

Cassandra gave her a look that told Robyn she was fooling no one with her "I'm okay" act. "Nick."

Robyn put her swatch aside. "It's not as if we were dating or anything." But it felt as though they'd been so much more to each other.

"No. The situation you were in was much more significant than mere dating," Cassandra said.

Robyn had thought that too at one time. Now she knew better. And she wasn't about to get her hopes up or her heart broken again by that reckless, adventure-loving playboy. Once had been quite enough, thank you very much. Aware Cassandra was still waiting for an explanation, Robyn murmured cagily, "Yes, well, you know Nick. He doesn't believe in love at first sight."

"Perhaps not until now," Cassandra said bluntly.

"Perhaps not, period."

Silence fell between the two of them. "Have you talked to him about anything but business since Nick took over as CEO?" Cassandra asked.

"No. And I don't really expect to." Robyn put the bolt of fabric she'd been holding into the "maybe" pile, and picked up another from the stack she was perusing.

"I don't know why not. It's obvious you're still deeply in love with him. Why don't you just level with him and tell him how you feel?

Robyn felt herself turn a fiery red. "I can't."

"Why not?"

Because I backed him into a corner once, when I kidnapped him. I won't do it again now, by telling him I love him. By making him feel obligated. "It wouldn't be fair to put him on the spot that way."

"It wouldn't be fair *not* to tell him," Cassandra disagreed.

"I think he knows how I feel," Robyn said softly, recalling their passionate kisses and the way she'd made love to him, with all her heart and soul. "And if he doesn't, it's probably because he doesn't want to know."

"I wouldn't be so sure of that." Cassandra turned with a smile. "Ah. Right on time, I see."

"Did you think I wouldn't be?" a familiar male voice drawled.

The sound of that low, sexy voice sending shivers of sensual awareness down her spine, Robyn looked toward the door and felt her heart skip not just one, but several beats. Nick was standing in the portal, resplendent in a black tuxedo. His ash blond hair was agreeably rumpled and his dark green eyes were alight with devilment any woman in her right mind would have found irresistible. He had a hot-pink water pistol in his hand. Whatever this was about, Robyn thought, amused despite her resolve not to be, it wasn't about Wyatt & Company business. This evening, Nick was at his sexy, mischievous best.

"Mother, I don't think you're needed here," Nick said in a voice that brooked no argument.

Cassandra grinned, as if she'd just had the biggest and best surprise of her entire life. "I can see I'm not." She slipped from the room, leaving Nick and Robyn very much alone.

Robyn planted her hands on her hips and faced him. She could feel the heat rushing to her face. Deep inside her, her heart slammed against her ribs. "What's this all about?" she demanded coolly.

Nick sent her a devil-may-care grin. "Let's just consider it a little payback," he promised.

"One good time deserves another?" Robyn guessed in the most level you-can't-just-come-in-here-and-sweep-me-off-my-feet voice.

"Something like that." Nick glanced down at the designs scattered across her desk and nodded approvingly. "Nice. Although I'd like to see *you* in a lot less."

"Nick!"

"Got your purse? Good. We'd better hurry," he said as he waved the hot-pink water pistol her way. "Joseito's waiting."

Memories of the last night the two of them had taken off at gunpoint flooding her senses, Robyn fell into step beside him. There was a roaring in her ears, and her throat was so tight she could hardly speak. "What does Joseito have to do with all of this?"

Nick shrugged and slid a hand around her back. He pulled her into the curve of his arm, as if she had never left it. "Can't have a kidnapping without him."

Robyn slowed her steps, afraid to hope, and yet unable to do anything but hope. "Nick," she said softly as her eyes beseeched his, "what does this mean?"

Nick grinned mysteriously. "You'll find out everything you need to know when you need to know it, and not a moment before," he promised in a cocky tone that brought back another flood of memories.

"Now where have I heard that before?" Robyn asked drolly. She was happier after having spent only two minutes with Nick than she had been in all the time without him.

They slipped into the elevator. "You look tired." He stepped nearer and rubbed his thumb across her cheek.

The possessive gesture sent a thrill spiraling down her spine, and generated warm heat inside her. "I haven't been getting a lot of sleep," Robyn confessed.

"Neither have I."

"That could be dangerous, when you're racing."

"Tell me about it." Nick rolled his eyes. "Which is why I've decided to give it up."

For a moment Robyn was so stunned she could barely breathe. "Racing?"

Nick nodded. The elevator doors opened. They rushed through the lobby and into the waiting limo at the curb. Joseito held the door for Robyn. He was grinning like a kid who'd just found Santa Claus.

"To tell you the truth," Nick continued, as he settled back onto the seat and poured them both some champagne. "I'm getting a little old for driving. I don't want to age like Andretti and the Unsers. It's time I move on to the next step."

"Which is?"

"Finding and backing other young drivers. I've met a lot of up-and-coming hotshots on the circuit. Most of them just need the chance to drive a top-quality car to be successful. I've talked to Mother about it, and she agrees it'd be a good way to bring some money back to Wyatt & Company, so we're going to start backing the drivers I select."

Robyn was quiet a long moment. "That's very generous of you, Nick."

"That's exactly what Mother said."

"But are you sure you won't miss driving yourself? I mean, I thought you liked all the travel, glamour, publicity, and excitement."

Nick grinned. "I still do. But Wyatt & Company has all that, too. In fact, I find our recent moves to expand and diversify the company particularly challenging and exciting. At last I found a way to meet my family obligations and be happy, too. But Wyatt & Company also has something that racing doesn't have. It has you, Robyn." He pulled her into his arms and delivered a lengthy kiss that packed more wallop than a roller coaster.

When the wildly sensual kiss had at last come to a halt and she could halfway think again, Robyn studied Nick's face. This was all she had ever wanted, more than she had dreamed possible. But what did Nick want? A way to continue his career as a race-car driver on another, higher level and a love affair on the side?

"Why are you looking so sad?" Nick asked as Robyn's spirits plummeted twice as quickly as they'd risen.

"Nothing," she lied.

"Does it have anything to do with me?" he asked.

Oh, Nick, you silly fool, Robyn thought, it has everything to do with you. *Tell him how you feel,* Cassandra had said. *Tell him you love him.* If she did that, she could be risking everything, Robyn knew. But if she didn't tell him, she'd never know how he felt.

"I love you." There, she had blurted it out.

Nick moved away from her abruptly, as if he could see her more clearly from a distance. "What?"

"I said I love you!" Robyn shouted, then flushed as Nick began to grin from ear to ear.

"Well, hey, I love you, too," he drawled, taking her back into his arms.

Robyn stared at him, looking so strong and vital and unutterably male beside her. "Then why didn't you tell me that?" she asked, thoroughly exasperated and deliriously happy all at once.

"Because I was confused," Nick said softly. "Everything had happened so fast. I didn't want to mix up what we were feeling then with all we'd been through.

So I took a few weeks to get back to my normal routine and cool off. And you know what?'' He traced the curve of her cheekbone with the back of his hand. ''Nothing changed. I still went to sleep every night thinking of you, I still dreamed about you every night, and I still woke up wishing I could see you outside of meetings and talk to you about more than just Wyatt & Company business. I still wished I could kiss you and hold you as close as I'm holding you now.'' He tightened his arms around her possessively.

''Oh, Nick.'' Robyn sighed as tears of pure bliss slid from the corners of her eyes. She buried her face in his chest, breathing in the wintery scent of him.

''And I thought you needed time, too,'' Nick said. ''To sort all this out.'' He tucked his hand beneath her chin and lifted her face to his. ''I wasn't wrong, was I? You were confused, too, weren't you?''

Robyn nodded, secure enough in his love for her to be honest with him. ''I know what I felt, what I wanted to be true, to happen, but I couldn't be sure about you. Couldn't be sure it wasn't simply the circumstances and not our hearts talking...''

''But now you know,'' Nick said softly, drinking in the sight of her face and holding her as if he never wanted to let her go. ''Now we both know. So there's only one thing to do about it.''

Robyn wasn't sure her heart could take any more surprises. ''And what, pray tell, might that be?'' she asked wryly, knowing from the adventurous smile on his lips that her Nick was anticipating something tremendously exciting and fulfilling.

''Get married,'' Nick said.

Robyn's heart soared.

"Which is why," he said as the limo pulled into Fort Worth's Alliance airport and headed for the hangar, "we're going back to our villa. You remember that church there in the valley?"

Robyn nodded.

"That's where I want to marry you," he said softly.

Tears of bliss filled her eyes. "Oh, Nick, you couldn't have picked a more perfect place. But what about our jobs?"

"Mother has already graciously agreed to handle everything until we get back. Besides, we have a whole lifetime to run Wyatt & Company when we return, but only one chance to be married and make it really special. And I do want to be married to you, Robyn," he whispered tenderly, "so very much."

"Oh, Nick, I want that, too," Robyn said, hugging him fiercely. She paused, knowing how Nick had always professed to be as unsentimental a guy as ever was. She regarded him curiously. "But why go all the way to Mexico when we could be married here—with probably a lot less trouble?"

Nick's eyes turned serious. "Because that's where it all began, because that's where I first fell in love with you. I couldn't think of a more perfect place for us to exchange our vows. I want to honeymoon there, too. That is, if it's okay with you."

How could she have ever thought Nick was unromantic? He had a sentimental streak in him a mile long, she thought, her whole body radiating the pleasure and contentment she felt, just being with him again. "Of course it's okay with me," she said, kissing him first sweetly, then with building intensity.

"Oh, Nick, we're finally going to be together," Robyn murmured with soft satisfaction, knowing she at last had all the romance, passion and excitement in her life she had ever wished for.

Nick nodded. "From this day forward, it's you and me, Robyn. We're never going to be apart again."

1993 Keepsake

CHRISTMAS

Stories

Capture the spirit and romance of Christmas with KEEPSAKE CHRISTMAS STORIES, a collection of three stories by favorite historical authors. The perfect Christmas gift!

Don't miss these heartwarming stories, available in November wherever Harlequin books are sold:

ONCE UPON A CHRISTMAS by Curtiss Ann Matlock
A FAIRYTALE SEASON by Marianne Willman
TIDINGS OF JOY by Victoria Pade

ADD A TOUCH OF ROMANCE TO YOUR HOLIDAY SEASON WITH KEEPSAKE CHRISTMAS STORIES!

HARLEQUIN®

AMERICAN ♦ ROMANCE®

Have Yourself an American Romance Christmas!

Christmas is the one time of year when dreams—no matter how small or how large—come true with a wish . . . and a kiss. In December, we're celebrating this spirit—and bringing our dashing heroes right under the mistletoe, just for you!

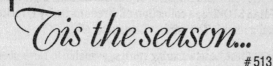

Tis the season...

#513
FALLING ANGEL
by Anne Stuart

#514
YES, VIRGINIA . . .
by Peg Sutherland

#515
NO ROOM AT THE INN
by Linda Randall Wisdom

#516
MERRY CHRISTMAS, BABY
by Pamela Browning

SEASON

Are you looking for more titles by

CATHY GILLEN THACKER

Don't miss these fabulous stories by one of
Harlequin's most renowned authors:

Harlequin American Romance®

#16367	IT'S ONLY TEMPORARY	$2.95	☐
#16388	FATHER OF THE BRIDE	$3.25	☐
#16407	AN UNEXPECTED FAMILY	$3.29	☐
#16423	TANGLED WEB	$3.29	☐
#16445	HOME FREE	$3.39	☐
#16452	ANYTHING'S POSSIBLE	$3.39	☐
#16456	THE COWBOY'S MISTRESS	$3.39	☐
#16472	HONEYMOON FOR HIRE	$3.39	☐
#16483	BEGUILED AGAIN	$3.39	☐
#16494	FIANCÉ FOR SALE	$3.50	☐

(limited quantities available on certain titles)

TOTAL AMOUNT	$	
POSTAGE & HANDLING	$	
($1.00 for one book, 50¢ for each additional)		
APPLICABLE TAXES*	$	_____
TOTAL PAYABLE	$	_____
(check or money order—please do not send cash)		

To order, complete this form and send it, along with a check or money order for the
total above, payable to Harlequin Books, to: *In the U.S.*: 3010 Walden Avenue,
P.O. Box 9047, Buffalo, NY 14269-9047; *In Canada*: P.O. Box 613, Fort Erie, Ontario,
L2A 5X3.

Name: _____

Address: _____City: _____

State/Prov.: _____Zip/Postal Code: _____

*New York residents remit applicable sales taxes.
Canadian residents remit applicable GST and provincial taxes.

HCGTBACK1

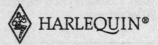

HARLEQUIN®